Gone to the Dogs

June Whyte

A Gumshoe Chicks Mystery
Book 1

White City
Press

Books by June Whyte

Sex on Tuesdays

THE GUMSHOE CHICK MYSTERY SERIES
Gone to the Dogs
For the Love of Dogs
Doggone It!

VETS 2U MYSTERY SERIES
Murder at Kangaroo Downs
Death at Dingo Creek
Homicide at Emu Lodge

KAT MCKINLEY GREYHOUND MYSTERIES
Chasing Can Be Murder
Muzzled
Hounded
Leashed

CHIANA RYAN CHILDREN'S MYSTERIES
The Case of the Disappearing Corpse
The Case of the Missing Dinosaur Egg

www.amazon.com/author/junewhytebooks

Gone to the Dogs

June Whyte

This edition published by White City Press
An imprint of Misti Media LLC
https://www.mistimedia.com
Available in both Paperback and eBook Editions
1 2 3 4 5 6 7 8 9 10
Text Copyright © June Whyte 2019
Paperback ISBN: 9781963479188
eBook ISBN: 9781963479089

GONE TO THE DOGS is dedicated to all the quirky, sweet, wonderful dogs that have made my life so much richer and more complete over the years. Especially you, YOLO. ☺

1

My name is Abigail Truelove and my life changed the day I discovered Petra Sullivan, my nemesis, was sleeping with the show judge.

The Ladies Kennel-Club was staging its Annual Championship dog show at the Royal Adelaide Showground and over the last four hours, two hundred or more competitors had stacked, primed, and shown off their dog's attributes to the presiding judges.

It was now down to the group finalists. Seven dogs, battling it out for the coveted Best in Show award. And as my smooth-haired dachshund, *Tempestuous Dawn* had won Best in Hound Group, I stood in the middle of the line-up, my dog stacked, alert, and ready.

An order from the judge sent the winner of the Gundog Group, the Honorable Lady Felicity Taylor, into instant action. She lifted her three chins high in the air and set off around the ring with her jet-black cocker spaniel in tow. God, that dog could move. Pity it didn't have a brain in its head. Not that it mattered. When it came to Best in Show material, surface beauty was all that counted.

Since joining the competitive show ranks, I'd learned that dog shows were akin to a battle ground. Like hard-fought wars, strategies to win that coveted Best in Show sash were planned with precision and dedication. Hours on the treadmill to keep up the dog's muscle-tone. Marathon do-overs with clippers, brushes and expensive beauty products. Secret diets passed down through generations of show families.

I'd inherited *Tempestuous Dawn* (aka Chloe, the most gorgeous and lovable dachshund on this earth) a year ago when my favorite relative, Aunt Tilly, died of a heart attack while kayaking in the North of Queensland. Not having children of her own, she also left me *Pampered Pooch,* an exclusive doggy boutique that sold designer-brand products on the High Street. At the time, my boyfriend, Luke, although happy with the money generated from the boutique, wasn't too keen on the canine edition to our family. He complained about the time I spent with the 'bloody dog' and pretended to be allergic to the minutest amount of dog hair left on the sofa. Right from the start, he'd advocated selling Chloe; said we'd get big bucks for the dog. But it wasn't going to happen. One – Aunt Tilly would rise up her from the grave if I dared put *Tempestuous Dawn* on the market. And two – I fell head over heels in love with the quirky little dog and decided I'd continue showing her. After all, this dog was a near-perfect specimen of the breed and under Aunt Tilly's expert handling had previously won Best in Show in every state of Australia.

Not that I'd enjoyed Aunt Tilly's success. At the first five shows I'd entered, Chloe had bombed. Dramatically. She hadn't even won her breed class.

But today, with the sound of crated dogs yapping from inside the pavilion and the overpowering scent of whichever new beauty product Lady Felicity had doused both herself and her cocker-spaniel, *Mein Freund Merry Widow,* I was determined to give it my best shot.

Lady Felicity, nose in the air, completed two laps of the ring and moved back into line with the other finalists. A total professional, she immediately presented her dog to the judge, head up, tail straight and four legs in perfect alignment. A twenty-year doyen of the game, the woman's show-ring skills and professional attire always went a long way towards collecting Best in Show ribbons.

While realigning Chloe's left ear so it sat in perfect placement to her right ear, I noticed my best friend Molly Gibson plucking nervously at the number tag pinned to her shirt. Molly had only joined the show dog ranks to keep me company. And although Busta, her smooth-coated Fox Terrier, absolutely loved to show off in the ring, Molly was happier in the background, helping to run the shows. This was the first time Busta had won Best Terrier in Group and by the way Molly was chewing on her fingernails, she wouldn't be opening any tricky butter-pats in the near future.

"Number twenty-six, lady with the smooth-haired dachshund, I'd like to see your dog's paces please." The judge, an older guy with a cowlick and shoes that were a little run down at the heels, nodded his head at me.

Again? God, this judge was taking more time to make up his mind than a group of politicians debating Climate Change.

I sucked in a quick steadying breath. "Okay, my love, let's show them what you can do." With a slight tug on Chloe's lead I stepped out of the line-up. Having already won Champion of Breed and Champion Hound, if I could keep Chloe's attention a little longer, she had a good chance of winning Best in Show.

Tempestuous Dawn floated across the ground with me powering along beside her, puffing like the little-engine-that-could. Understandable, considering I'd scarfed an entire block of Rocky Road chocolate, plus a large packet of M&Ms before entering the ring – show-nerves – so by the time we moved back into line, the sweat welling on my face was doing a pretty good job of removing my makeup.

But the moment we came to a halt, Chloe began to sag.

"No, no, no. Only a couple more minutes," I whispered, trying valiantly to keep her stumpy little legs from folding, while silently willing the judge to get his ass into gear and make a decision.

"Sorreee…I got held up in the Little Girls Room."

I blinked in surprise as the shark of the show-world, Petra Sullivan, bee-stung lips the color of old plasma, and hot pink jeans so tight you could define every delineation of her *hoo-ha*, sashayed into the show-ring, her overweight pug, the dubious winner of the Toy Group, dragging along behind her.

"Hey, you can't waltz in here now, you're too late!" I hissed through gritted teeth as Petra stopped in front of me to adjust one of her overflowing boobs.

How did she even get past the steward at the gate?

Petra's grin was so smarmy it would curdle yoghurt. She gave a tiny shoulder-shrug in response, then proceeded to push her way into first-cab-off-the-rank position at the top of the line-up. All the while ignoring the snorts of anger from the handlers of the other six Group winners.

Surely, Mr. Oliver Hutchins, who purported to have judged at big shows in both England and America, would order the gate-crasher out of the ring. This class had been in progress for half an hour. The judge was on the brink of announcing his winner. No way could a contestant enter the ring and be judged once a class was in action.

The rules were in black and white.

All eyes swiveled from Perky Petra to Mr. Procrastination. All waiting in anticipation for the interloper to be tossed out on her well-defined derriere. But nothing happened. Not a crumb of censure passed the esteemed judge's lips. No steward came to drag Petra out of the ring by her ultra-long false eyelashes. Instead, Oliver T. Hutchins grew an inch or two taller, sucked in his stomach and straightened his bow-tie. All the while beaming at the latest competitor as though she was a double decker chocolate-swirl ice-cream and he couldn't wait to lick her.

Had he been stalling? Waiting for Petra to enter the ring? Was that why he'd been taking so long to announce his winner?

At first, when the whispers skittered along the line-up that Petra was *doing* the judge, I couldn't believe it. That is, until Petra threw a little finger wave in the direction of Mr. Easily-Swayed and he answered with a suggestive lick of his lips and an almost imperceptible pelvic thrust. *A pelvic thrust?* At his age? I could feel the ire churning around in my chest, escalating with every spin and preparing to explode via my mouth with a few well-chosen, but completely unladylike words. Pitched at a very high volume. Hey, I'd been the bunny who'd spent hours on the phone with this guy as a representative of the Ladies Kennel Club. I'd been the one who'd pleaded and offered him more money than our club could afford to pay for his services.

Silly me…I'd got it wrong.

I'd stroked the guy's ego while Petra stroked his whatnot.

As I watched the judge swagger across the ring, his eyes lasering in on the pair of double D's escaping from the front of Petra's low-cut blouse, I knew we'd missed the boat.

Chloe must have sensed it too. Weary of all this standing around looking suave and beautiful, she decided it was way past her nap time. She dug several pivots out of the grass, turned three times on the spot, curled up in a ball and promptly fell sleep.

I didn't bother waking her. What was the point? Even considered the merits of joining her.

The judge, after sending Petra and *Princess Sauvignon of Glenville* for one measly lap of the ring, pulled the fat little pug out of the line-up and presented Petra with a trophy and the coveted multi-colored Best in Show sash.

Unbelievable.

The moment Petra exited the ring, the other six Group winners rounded on her. For a split second, I actually felt sorry for the woman. But only for a split second.

"You conniving little tart!" Steven Channing, owner of the Non-Sporting Group winner, a beautifully trimmed-and-primped-to-within-an-inch-of-its-life apricot Standard Poodle, *Supreme Champion Windswept Fly By Me*, who'd won more Best in Show ribbons than most dogs had breakfasts, got right up into her face. His gold medallion, ear rings and matching necklace vibrating with his anger. "You bitch! You slept with him, didn't you?"

Petra wrinkled her nose. "Back up, Stevie. Your breath smells like you've been sucking on some guy's…dirty socks."

"Stone the flamin' crows!" snarled Wild Bill Hooter, the bearded winner of the Working Dog group. "Stephen's right. You're nothing but a tart!" He spat a lump of phlegm in Petra's direction, completely ignoring his Border Collie who was attempting to hump Petra's pug.

"*I'm* lodging a formal complaint to the committee." Lady Felicity snatched up her Cocker Spaniel who was also showing interest in Petra's pop-eyed pug and stormed off in the direction of the Secretary's office.

The accusations fell on deaf ears.

Petra, all smiles, shimmied a path through the angry contestants, all the while flapping her Best in Show ribbon in our faces, like a matador waving a red cape at a bull.

"What I don't understand is how you could *do* that, Petra? How you could climb into bed with a guy old enough to be your father, a guy you don't even know – just to win a ribbon?" That was Molly, my best friend. Of course, Molly's views on sex were a little out-dated. Like a marriage certificate in full view on the bed-side table and even then, nothing more erotic than the missionary position while lying back and *doing it for England.*

Over the years, I'd tried to drag my friend into the 21st Century, but it was a hard-uphill slog. Probably because Molly's parents died in a car crash when she was four and she'd been brought up by her strict Great-Granny Teresa, whose archaic ideas of carnality meant the actual word *sex* hadn't been invented yet.

There was a scuffle at my feet. I looked down and let out a laugh. Busta, Molly's exuberant Fox Terrier knew *exactly* what the word sex meant. He was going hammer-and-tongs on top of *Princess Sauvignon of Glenville* like it was Christmas morning and Santa had left the little pug under the tree, all boxed and gift-wrapped, just for him.

Petra's laugh was breathy, almost a snigger. "You're *so* naïve, Molly. It's almost as if you never left high school."

"But you didn't answer her question," I said, bending to help my friend extricate Busta from his carnal bliss before facing up to Petra.

"That's easy. I *adore* sex." Petra flicked her shoulder-length bottle-blonde hair over her shoulder as if that explained everything. "And if being horny gets me what I want in life, why not?"

I shoved Busta into Molly's arms and turned back to Petra. "Even if it means cheating?"

"Prove it."

"I intend to."

Petra barked out a laugh. "Oh, Abi, do you honestly believe Mr. Please-Pass-the-Viagra would admit to having sex in return for favours rendered. If so, you're as delusional as your weird friend." She eyed the accusing faces around her, all hanging on to her every word. "You know, if I divulged the names of all the guys I've slept with – just this month – at least *one* of you losers would be booting your other-half out of the cosy love-nest." As she spoke, her hard eyes, glinting with malice, zeroed in on me.

"What do you mean?" My voice came out strangled, as though a lump the size of a tennis ball had lodged in my throat. "What are you implying?"

Molly touched my arm. "Come on, Abi, she's just winding you up."

"I'm *implying* nothing." Petra stepped closer, a smirk thickening her cosmetically full-blown lips. "All I'm saying is *maybe* some men prefer to suck on juicy watermelons instead of–" she tipped her head forward and blatantly studied my chest. "–sour little lemons? And *maybe* some men look forward to fireworks in bed, instead of damp squibs."

I shrugged off Molly's restraining hand, a bitter taste of bile flooding my mouth. Was Luke really having it off with Petra? Was that why he seemed a little preoccupied, lately? Accusing me of not trusting him? Telling me I was too clingy?

Well, if this was a test – he'd failed miserably. It proved I was right all along not to trust him.

Or was Petra lying?

"If I find out you've been in bed with Luke," I growled, grabbing hold of Petra's arm and swinging her around, forcibly holding back from planting a fist into that smirking face. "I'll dice you into little pieces and feed you to the sea-gulls."

"Oh, dear, always so dramatic." Petra pulled away and laughed. "If it helps, *darling*, sex means nothing to me. It's just a bit of fun. Like scratching an itch."

My nails bit into my palms as my fists tightened.

"Come on, Abi, don't let her get to you," Molly broke in, dragging me away, her face pale. I took my eyes off Petra long enough to glance across at my best friend. Molly looked upset. Sick. She had that haunted expression on her face – the one that said, '*Oh, God, it looks like a fight… and I'm so not into fisticuffs or hair-pulling because I'll be the one who ends up in hospital or paying for a new hairstyle to cover the gaps in my hair.*'

"But Petra slept with Luke."

"She's winding you up. Can't you see that? No way would Luke cheat on you." Molly's grip on my arm tightened. "Especially with a woman who treats sex like an Extreme Olympic Sport. Luke loves you."

All the red-hot anger crashing around inside my chest suddenly abated and dribbled away. "Does he?" I could hear the wobble in my voice. "That's the problem, Molly. I'm not so sure he does."

2

Fifteen minutes later, Chloe and Busta settled happily into their personal crates, Molly and I met up with our other bestie, Dana, in the refuge of the dog pavilion's cavernous cafeteria. I wasn't hungry, but Molly was determined to find somewhere to talk, and, as judging was officially over for the day, the cafeteria was almost empty. Only a sprinkling of show-competitors sat at the tables eating or drinking a final coffee. The rest were still in the pavilion, frantically dismantling grooming stands, re-packing gear and loading it all into personally fitted-out cars and vans before driving home.

Only to repeat the madness again at another venue the following weekend.

Molly claimed an empty table hugging the rear wall of the cafeteria and furthest from the clatter of eager-to-finish-for-the-day staff who were busy collecting trays, clearing tables and stacking chairs. "Okay," she said, her voice determined, "out with it, Abi. What makes you think Luke doesn't love you?"

Coffee in one hand and a custard tart in the other, I eased into the chair next to her and sighed. I wasn't ready to divulge the petty squabbles, how distant Luke had become, the days when he barely answered when I spoke. Not yet, anyway. Instead, I lifted one sardonic eyebrow at Molly, hoping to divert her questions. "Well, for a start, my boyfriend of almost two years, the man I live with, had it off with Petra bloody Sullivan. You know, the woman who'd jump into bed with a goat if she thought it would help her cause? Pretty good reason to suspect he doesn't love me, don't you think?" I pushed the sugar bowl across the table to my other best friend, Dana Fox, owner of Penelope, one of the gentlest greyhounds to grace the show-ring, and the third member of our tightly knit threesome.

The three of us had become firm friends in the seventh grade, when Molly's bicycle was stolen. The local police, with more important crimes on their to-do list, weren't overly interested, so we decided it was up to us to find the culprit and reclaim Molly's bike. And we did. A dodgy guy was going around stealing bikes, repainting them in a different color and selling them on eBay to pay for his alcohol obsession. With that success under our tunic belts, we decided we'd team up to fight Good against Evil.

Of course, we needed a signature name, so, while toying with *Nancy Drew Apprentices* and *The Three Sherlocks,* we discovered a bundle of old crime novels that used to belong to Molly's great-grandmother. In these books, the private detectives were known as *gumshoes.*

Hence, *The Gumshoe Chicks* were born.

After this we went on to solve several school-yard mysteries, but once we'd graduated from High School and were confronted with the three big ones in life – dating, working for a living, and responsibilities – although our friendship grew stronger, the investigations fizzled out.

I watched Dana spoon four heaped teaspoons of sugar into her cup of weak black tea and waited for her to stick her oar into the conversation. It didn't take long. "I don't know why you're so uptight, Abi," she said. "You *know* you can't trust a word that tramp says. Petra would have everyone believe she slept with Chris Hemsworth, if she thought she could get away with it."

"But what if she *is* telling the truth? What if Luke, you know, was feeling a bit *off* me one day, or we'd had a tiff about, I don't know…" I shrugged, "…the three hundred dollars I paid for that stunning new rhinestone collar I bought for Chloe the other week? And what if Petra sashayed up our driveway wearing nothing but a black lacy garter belt underneath her trench coat? And what if, when Luke invited her in, she undid the buttons slowly and let her coat puddle onto the floor? And what if–"

"Abi, just listen to yourself, will you? You know Petra is a chronic liar. Forget what she said about Luke. Just go home, order his favorite take-away, make marathon love to him, and put her poison out of your mind."

The thought of Luke's hands – and lips – all over Petra's naked body, made me want to puke. I pushed my custard tart away, untouched. "I can't make love to Luke again until I know the truth."

"Codswallop! Now you're being melodramatic." Dana nodded at the custard pie. "You eating that?" When I shook her head, she dragged the plate across the table and lined it up next to her large slice of apple pie. Fair dinkum, Dana was a freak of nature. Although she'd given birth to two children, she could eat all day long and never show signs of putting on weight, whereas I had to count every damn calorie that went into my mouth.

Molly, who'd been biding her time up until now, frowned as she placed her coffee cup squarely back onto its saucer. "You know, if it was me, I'd just *ask* Luke straight out and watch his body language when he answered."

Dana shook her head. "No, Moll. Bad suggestion. Accusing your boyfriend of cheating, without both photographic and audio proof, is a definite no-no." She gave Molly an exasperated eye roll. "It's no wonder you can't hang onto a guy. You need to learn to be more subtle, more devious in your techniques."

Plus, Molly's refusal to surrender her virginity without the legality of a marriage vow sent most guys calling for the nearest Uber and driving off into the sunset without her.

Molly gave a tiny shoulder-shrug. "Well, I'm sorry, but I don't get it. If Abi can't confront Luke, how is she supposed to find out if he's cheating or not?"

I was definitely with Molly on this one. "Yes, Dana. Spill."

Dana wiped custard from her mouth with the back of one hand and licked her lips. "Well, if it was me…"

I stifled a laugh. "This should be interesting." *Dana Fox, the married-with-two-kids member of our threesome, was about to divulge one of her many secrets on how to run her own dog-wash franchise, be a hands-on mum and still find time to keep her man from straying.*

"I'd employ a private investigator to follow him, see what he's up to."

"You're joking," I said with a laugh. "Your big secret is for me to pay someone to follow Luke?"

"Why not? Get *hard* evidence to slap down in front of the piece of shit when he denies everything. Only way."

"Surely it would be easier *and* less costly just to ask him if he's done the deed with Petra. I know when Luke's lying. He blinks and bites his bottom lip. It's always a tell."

"How do you know he's not just nervous. Think about it, when you're nervous you scratch behind your left ear. And you do exactly the same thing when you're lying."

"Do not!"

"Yes, you do." Dana fossicked around in her large over-the-shoulder red leather handbag. After depositing a rather-worse-for-wear gray toy donkey with a limp green and white spotted bow tie on the table, together with a large unopened bag of baby-wipes, she dragged out her cell and began scrolling. Then, after clicking on a number, she held the phone out to me. "Here. This guy's a P.I. He opens his office every third Sunday for those who work during the week, so he'll be there tomorrow. And believe me, as well as being better looking than God, he takes no prisoners."

What? I waved both hands in a *no-way* gesture. I didn't know what to say to a P.I. And even if I did – I couldn't afford to hire one.

Ignoring me, Dana forced the phone into my hands, then sat back, head to one side, arms folded.

"Umm…"

"Stevens & Forrester Private Investigators. Good afternoon, Nathan Forrester speaking." The voice on the other end of the phone was deep, rich, like honeyed chocolate. "And what can I do for you, today, Madam?"

Good question…

Now if only I could persuade my squeaky voice to work, I might even drum up a good answer.

*****

The office I entered the following afternoon was nothing like I'd expected.

Okay, maybe I'd read too many of my mother's well-thumbed Raymond Chandler detective novels over the years, so my expectations were a few decades out of date. I looked around. There was no scratched desk, stained with coffee cup rings. No down-at-heel P.I., the epitome of a cagey, hard-boiled private detective with his feet on the desk and smoke curling from a chomped-on cigarette. And the man sitting behind the large chrome desk was typing on his laptop, not undressing me with his eyes, while thinking – '*It was a blonde. A blonde to make a bishop kick a hole in a stained-glass window…*'

Instead, Nathan Forrester looked up from his open laptop and smiled at me. A smile that made my legs go weak. A smile that could have a girl reaching for her latest Mills & Boon novel so she could get lost in the pages. With his jet-black hair, thick, shiny and well cut, he was a few years older than me, say early to mid-thirties, and judging by the muscle tone under his well-fitting shirt, he either led a very active sports life away from the office, or was a regular visitor to the gym. The coat of his silver-gray suit hung neatly on the back of his chair and his tie had been slightly loosened.

"Ms. Truelove?" And there was that lovely rich honeyed-chocolate voice I'd heard over the phone.

I nodded, checking for any signs of the usual veiled snigger I got whenever I gave my name, especially to the male species. There was none. Instead, he stood up and moved purposefully around the desk, right hand outstretched. "Lovely to meet you."

His hand closed over mine and unlike a lot of men who are afraid to really take a good grip on a woman's hand, his handshake was firm. In truth, it was electric. Like I'd plugged my fingers into a power socket. "Could I tempt you with a coffee?"

When I nodded, he smiled again. "Our coffee's not as good as Starbucks, I'm afraid, but I've tasted a lot worse." He strode across the room to where an industrial coffee-machine bubbled away quietly beside a small refrigerator and bent down to open a cupboard door. A movement I eyed with pleasure. He removed two dainty cups and saucers that wouldn't have lasted a week in my hands. Once he'd filled the cups, he placed a chocolate biscuit in the shape of a koala bear on each saucer. "Let's just say I drink at least *ten* of these a day and haven't developed any major intestinal problems, as yet."

"Good to know," I said. "But maybe, if you brought a large mug to work, you wouldn't need so many coffee breaks."

He grinned and indicated the adjoining room with a nod of his head. "Tried that once, but the dragon-lady who runs my office and sees that everything is as it should be, said clients prefer fine china."

After handing me a coffee, he settled back into his large leather chair, straightened his shoulders, and opened a notebook beside his laptop. He picked up a silver biro and tapped it against the blank page while studying me. "You mentioned on the phone you were interested in having your boyfriend, Luke Brody, investigated. You think he's cheating on you. Is that correct?"

Geez, that made me sound like an overly obsessive girlfriend. How had I let Dana talk me into this? I'd drink my coffee, eat that yummy looking chocolate biscuit and sneak out while the hunky PI was pouring himself a second cup. Fingers fidgeting with the delicate handle of the Dresden China cup, I told him about Petra's unethical behavior at the dog show and how the woman had also boasted that she'd slept with Luke.

"God, listening to myself, I'm not sure I have any grounds to go ahead with this investigation." I pulled a face and sighed. "It's just that I'd hate to accuse Luke of cheating if he's innocent."

"I see." He took a sip of his coffee and pushed the notebook away. "Dana Fox talked you into coming to see me, did she?"

I nodded.

"Thought so. Her number showed up when you rang me yesterday."

"Well–"

"Did Dana also mention I'm a good friend of her husband from University days and therefore conducted her investigation for free?"

I frowned. All Dana had *mentioned* was she'd used Nathan Forrester of Stevens & Forrester to check on her husband, Peter, six months ago. She thought he was cheating on her – only to discover the woman he'd been seeing three times a week for a month was a piano-teacher who'd been coaching him to play a simplified version of *As Long as you Love Me* from the *Backstreet Boys*. It was Dana's favorite song and Peter wanted to surprise his wife by playing and singing it for her at the Red Lion, a Club where they'd booked a table for their fifth anniversary dinner.

"When Dana came to see me earlier this year," Forrester said, breaking into my thoughts. "I was bowled over when she told me she thought Peter was cheating on her. They're made for each other those two, and with two adorable kids, I didn't want to see the family unit broken up due to a misunderstanding." He loosened his tie a little more. "I also knew Dana couldn't afford our fees, so, being a friend of Peter's, I did the investigation in my own time, for free."

"Hmm…can't say she brought up the word *free* in any of our conversations."

His lips twitched. "And I don't suppose she mentioned that we normally charge our clients $300 an hour to look into their claims. *And* that our investigations usually take, on average, 24 billed hours to complete?"

Holy hens' teeth!

I tried to add that up in my head. 300 x 24. Couldn't get past the 300 x 4 is $1,200 without the 300 x 20 to add on to that. "You know, maybe I should just think about this for a few days, Mr. Forrester, and get back to you."

"Sensible idea. And call me Nathan. My father's name is Mr. Forrester."

I looked up from the depths of the coffee I was studying like it was a complicated trigonometry equation to find him watching me. His eyes were the color of the sea on a crisp winter morning. I hadn't noticed that when I first walked in. "You know, maybe I'll just *ask* Luke." I gave a nervous laugh and waved the little chocolate koala biscuit in the air before biting off its head. "Who knows, he might even get a laugh out of the whole Petra thing."

"I agree."

I studied the man on the other side of the desk, noting the way his shoulders strained against the confines of his duck-egg blue shirt. He took another sip of his coffee and smiled at me. A smile that did funny things to my lady bits. Warm, uninhibited things. Yep. This guy was definitely like rich honey-centered chocolate. And I was totally addicted to chocolate.

Time to end this consultation and get the hell out of his office before I took a huge bite out of Mills & Boon's pin-up poster, Mr. Nathan Forrester.

He laced his fingers together, eyes never leaving mine. "I think it's always wise to confront the other person in a situation like this. If your Luke really loves you, he'll go out of his way to prove his fidelity."

"And if he *has* been sleeping with Petra?"

"Then I'll be free to ask you out to dinner."

A mouthful of coffee, halfway down my throat, did an *oh-shit!* and spurted back up again. All over Nathan's nicely polished desk.

He ignored the spilt coffee and as I pushed myself out of the chair, handed me a business card. "Good luck with Luke, but if he's been cheating on you, ring me. You deserve better than that, Abigail Truelove."

Nodding like a bobble-headed dog, I snared the remainder of my chocolate koala biscuit, pocketed Nathan's business card and almost tripped over my feet in my hurry to get away.

Real ladylike, Abi, I muttered as I sprinted down the stairs. *A good-looking guy with both manners and money makes a pass at you and you act like a Victorian airhead.*

3

We were on a stakeout. Dana's idea, of course. But when I told her the cost of employing a registered PI, who wasn't a friend of the family, she'd decided we could do just as good a job ourselves. For nothing more than the cost of some potato chips and nibbles.

'It's time the *Gumshoe Chicks* dusted off their sleuthing capes, dug out their fingerprint powder and came out of retirement,' she'd declared waving her hand around like a magician procuring a rabbit out of a hat.

However, we were fast learning that stakeouts weren't for sissies. Stuck in a car for hours, twiddling thumbs, trying to stay awake, wasn't as exciting as it was made out to be in all those PI mystery novels I'd borrowed from the library over the years.

Guess that's why the books were shelved in the fiction section.

I took another long guzzle from my water bottle. I'd been stuffing my face with salt-and-vinegar crisps for the last two hours – more from boredom than an obsession with crisps – and now I was so thirsty I could drink the Port River dry.

"This is *so* boring." I wriggled in my seat to relieve my numb bum before screwing the stopper back on the water bottle and stowing it in the middle console of my van. "Nothing's happening."

"Surveillance is all about patience," Dana reminded me in that prissy voice she often used to reinforce the fact that she was the eldest by two months. "Patience and observation."

"But mainly, boredom," I reiterated.

"*And* stiffness," added Molly from the back seat where she was curled up with both Busta, her fox terrier and Penelope, Dana's greyhound, which as usual, wore a colorful bandana made in the same material as the shirts worn by Dana's two children. Tonight, it featured dragons and little prancing reindeers.

It was two hours since we'd parked my van over the road from *The Pussycat Parlor*, a nightclub situated in one of the back streets of Port Adelaide. Two hours spent watching people go in and out of the club. But up until now, the most exciting event we'd witnessed was a fall-down drunk who'd tripped over the gutter and plunged face-first into the pavement. His bucket of hot chips went spewing every which way onto the ground. Unperturbed, he lumbered to his knees and crawled around in the dirt until every last chip was picked up, dusted off and placed back into its cardboard container. Then, satisfied he'd rescued them all, he'd shuffled off down the street, continuing to eat his meal.

"This is a waste of time," I shook my head to emphasize the point. "Just because Petra's inside the nightclub, probably having a blast with someone else's boyfriend, I can't see how that's going to help our investigation."

"Think about it. Luke wasn't home when you left, Petra's inside a club of ill-repute, maybe they'll meet up in there and you'll get your answer. We've already photographed Petra going in and if Luke turns up, we'll catch him out too." Dana was head down, fossicking inside her family-sized leather hand-bag. Finally, she extricated a big blue pacifier, dipped it into a jar of honey, plugged it into her fifteen-month old son's open mouth and the bawling noise he'd been making for the last five minutes, stopped. The silence was greeted by three heart-felt sighs of relief.

Honestly, that kid could bawl for Australia.

If there was an International Bawling Competition judged purely on the decibels of the noise, Jake Fox would be a shoo-in to win the gold trophy.

"Any of those salt-and-vinegar crisps left?" asked Molly leaning over to check on the dwindling supply of nibbles.

"Here, take these." I passed an unopened packet of crisps over while dodging Busta, Molly's fox terrier's long exploratory tongue as he tried to lick the salt off my face. "Damn crisps made me so thirsty I emptied two full bottles of water. Now I need to use the restroom."

"Don't worry, I brought a bucket along for just such emergencies," said Molly, cheerfully.

"I'd rather burst."

"We promise not to watch you."

I rolled my eyes.

"Why don't you ask the doorman if he'll let you use the restroom inside the club?" Dana suggested. "You're good at fluttering your eye-lashes and looking adorably cute."

"Good idea. Anything's better than peeing in a bucket in the back of the van. Especially with seven pairs of eyes – including the dogs – trained on my every movement and seven pairs of ears listening to the sound effects."

"Wanna wee-wee too, Mummy. Really, really, *really* bad." Dana's other child, three-year-old Kayla, who'd been asleep up until now, began jigging up and down in her seat. "I go with Aunty Abi?"

Kayla, my godchild, was a sweetheart and I loved her dearly, but bringing two children under four on surveillance, when it was past their bed time, wasn't Dana's most brilliant move. However, tonight was Peter's night for playing poker with the boys, so she had little option. If it was up to me, Peter would be playing poker with the boys while bouncing Jake on his knee and watching Kayla play Angry Birds on his phone.

But that was just me…

"Sorry, sweet-pea. The doorman might let *me* in to use the restroom but there's no way he'll allow a three-year-old inside." I gently pushed my dog, Chloe, who'd been curled up fast asleep on my lap, onto the floor, opened the van door and extricated myself from behind the wheel. It was pure heaven to stretch my legs and shake the kinks out of my body. How registered Private Investigators could do this day in day out, I couldn't fathom. No wonder they charged $300 an hour.

Kayla's bottom lip dropped, and big fat tears edged the corner of her eyes. "B-but I w-wanna go with Aunty Abi."

"No, no, don't cry, darlin'." I hated it when Kayla cried. Made me go all teary too. With a smothered sniffle, I lifted her down onto the footpath, took her hand in mine and shrugged up at Dana. "Look, I'll ask the doorman, see what he says. If he refuses to let Kayla in, I'll bring her back, okay?" I grinned. "But if we *do* get the all-clear, don't worry, I won't let any of those nasty Pussies anywhere near her."

"You'd better not!"

"But I love pussy-cats, Aunty Abi. Can we pat one when we go inside? Please?"

"Umm…these pussies don't like being patted." I looked down into that angelic little face as we approached the front door of the club. *Don't grow up, Kayla, stay a little girl forever. Life's much simpler.* "They're all asleep, sweetheart, and sometimes pussy cats can get really mean when they're woken up."

The bouncer on the door, Boris, according to his name-tag, had muscles growing on top of his muscles but he also had a soft side and when I explained our predicament, he let us in on the proviso we were quick and didn't venture any further than the restroom.

"Betta tiptoe, Aunty Abi," whispered Kayla as we whooshed through the front door and headed down a narrow passageway. "We don't wanna wake up the pussies, do we?"

We certainly did not…

Toilet ablutions completed I led Kayla over to the sink to wash her hands just as the restroom door crashed open with such force it bounced off the wall. A young woman, no older than eighteen and dressed in little more than a flashy handkerchief and knee-high red suede boots staggered into the room, face behind the thick makeup whiter than Tiptop bread. Moaning, the girl barely made it into the nearest cubicle before throwing up.

"Pretty boots," said Kayla as I turned on the wall-drier to not only dry our hands, but also to drown out the noise of vomiting coming from behind the cubicle door.

To distract her, I grabbed Kayla's hand and, pretending to be a kangaroo, hopped across the room while the three-year-old, always ready to join in a game, copied me. Bounding through the restroom door back into the narrow passageway, the loud music from the club shook the walls each side of us and thudded through the ceiling.

"Come on, sweet-pea," I shouted over the din. "Let's get you out of here."

On the way to the exit, Kayla spotted two giant cat statues, one covered in artificial black fur and the other a gray tabby. The cats lounged like royalty, one each side of an open doorway, eyes wide, playful smiles etched on their faces. Evidently used as logos to advertise the nightclub.

Squealing with delight, Kayla pulled away from me and threw herself at the black cat, hugging it tightly. "These pussies not mean," she told me in her most grown-up voice. "They want to be our friends."

While Kayla was busy hugging, kissing, and discussing 'the sick lady with the pretty boots' with the two cat statues, I poked my head through the open doorway. Just for a quick peek. Okay, I'd heard lewd stories about *The Pussycat Parlor*, where dancers, strippers and pole-dancers earned a good living via tips from customers, but I'd never actually been inside the nightclub and couldn't resist checking it out for myself.

It was quite a spectacle.

Showy babes and gel-slicked guys were either getting smashed via tequila shots or on the prowl, while disco lights flickered on and off, turning hyped-up faces from pink, to blue, to iridescent green. The miniscule dance floor, a prime sexual marketplace, was jammed with swaying couples, their bodies locked together so closely a tissue would have trouble passing between them. And on the stage, three well-oiled pole-dancers were busy earning their tips.

Wow, did those girls have some innovative moves. They had to be double-jointed to perform at that level. Not only were they twisting their bodies into unnatural shapes, but the way they arched their body backward while sliding up and down the pole made my back ache, just watching them.

Eyes on the flexible performer working the middle pole, I blinked and did a double take. It was Petra Sullivan. I blinked again. What was my nemesis doing here, making-out on a greased pole? Dressed in nothing but a gold lamé thong, her blonde hair streaked with pink and silver and teased into a high beehive, her nipples spray painted in gold, Petra caressed the pole with her body as though she was in bed with a lover.

The Pussy Cat Parlor's star attraction.

And there, parked no more than five feet from the entertainment, following Petra's every move, was yesterday's show-judge, Oliver T. Hutchins. He wasn't dressed for clubbing. In fact, in his crisp white shirt, old-school tie and sharp three-piece suit, he looked like he'd be more at home at the opera.

But even in the dim light of the nightclub, I could see the fisted hands and the twisted scowl. And then, staring directly at Petra, he mouthed the words, "I'll kill you; you bitch!"

4

An hour later, after dropping Dana and Molly, plus kids and dogs off at their respective front gates, I pulled into the driveway of 138 Pennington Road, the two-bedroomed, one-bathroom home Aunt Tilly had left me in her will. The house Luke and I had shared for the last sixteen months.

After discovering Petra was working at the club and not actively engaged in stealing boyfriends, we'd decided there was little point in extending the stake-out any longer. Plus, baby Jake had started howling again. And he wouldn't stop. No amount of honey-covered pacifier, rocking from Dana, or kisses from Penelope, the greyhound, were having any effect on lowering the decibels. It was either go home and settle Jake down in his own cot or find ourselves questioned by the police or even a social worker.

I switched off the engine, extinguished the headlights and removed the keys from the ignition. But I was in no hurry to go inside. Instead, I sat staring through the windscreen at the rose bushes which lined the driveway. Barely distinguishable in the dark. Why was Petra working at The Pussycat Parlor for tips? Her Dad was in real estate. Her mum a rich socialite who'd inherited big money when her parents died. Petra, being an only child, had never had to work or worry about money before. Why now?

And what was Oliver T Hutchins, the supposedly well-credentialed show-judge doing at a dive like the Pussycat Parlor? Why was he angry? Had Petra threatened to come clean and inform the Ladies Kennel Club he and Petra had participated in sex for favors? Or maybe she'd decided it might be fun to secretly video their sex-romp and put it up on YouTube – just for a laugh?

As I closed and locked the car door then let Chloe off the lead to water the lawn before going inside, I took a deep breath. Steeled myself for the inevitable. If Oliver Hutchins wanted to play with fire by getting involved with Pussycat Petra, that was his problem. Not mine.

My problem lay inside the house.

Yep. It was time to face up to Luke and find out if we were still in a relationship. Find out if he'd had sex with my worst enemy. I couldn't put it off any longer. Stalking Petra in the hope she'd lead me to Luke was always going to be a waste of time.

I needed to pull up my big girl pants and confront him.

Now. Tonight.

I'd first met Luke Brody at a football match around two years ago. Not being a football fan myself, I'd been there under sufferance. It was my dad's birthday, so I'd not only bought him tickets to the Grand Final but also promised to accompany him to the match. My dad was a staunch Port Power fan and this scruffy but hot looking guy, with the head of a dragon tattooed on the back of his neck – I later discovered the rest of the dragon went all the way down his back and the scaly tail slashed across his very fine backside – sat on the seat next to me. Tattoo Guy was dressed head to toe in the opposite team's colors and during the match, countered every one of my weak, 'Go the Power!' contributions with an over-loud, 'Onya Crows!'

When he became more enthusiastic with his barracking, I told him *it was only a game,* so when the match finished, he'd invited me out to dinner. In his words, *'so I can explain to you, in minute detail, how football is NEVER just a game.'*

And somehow, although having very little in common, we'd become an item very quickly. Maybe it was the mind-blowing sex. Or the need to belong. Then, six months later, Luke shifted into Aunt Tilly's house with me.

We were an odd couple, but as the saying goes, opposites attract. Although, I had to admit, it made for some loud disagreements. I was inclined to be a bit of a neatnik – Luke couldn't even locate his sock drawer. I loved animals and often brought home strays – Luke thought they took too much of my attention away from him and quickly found new homes for them. I closed my eyes if the price tag on an article I *really* wanted was a little high – Luke was a cheapskate. Well, that's what I called him in the middle of an argument, whereas he preferred to label himself as 'thrifty.'

But our make-up sex was always worth the angst. Until recently. In fact, thinking about it, I realized we hadn't had sex for over two months. Luke was either too tired, too busy, too grumpy, or our disagreements had turned into cold-shoulder treatments.

Girding my loins, as self-help books suggest you do in times of stress, I whistled to Chloe and used my shoulder to open the front door while weighed down by a bag of left-over nibbles, an iPad, the remainder of Chloe's treats and a brown paper bag containing two Big Macs which I couldn't resist when we'd spotted a McDonalds on the way home. I figured if Luke was innocent and became angry after I accused him of sleeping with Petra, I'd share them with him to sweeten him up. And if he admitted to being involved with Petra, I'd shove both burgers down his throat and leave him there to choke while I stormed back to *The Pussycat Parlor* and used my bare hands on Petra's neck to achieve the same result.

As I walked in, I could hear the TV blaring in the lounge room, tuned into some football game. Of course. I'd soon discovered Luke was addicted to watching and betting on football, didn't matter which team, as long as there was an egg-shaped ball, an umpire to scream at and guys dressed in short shorts and colored jumpers involved. It was okay. It really was. Meant I could set up my own little tv in the spare room together with a comfortable lounge chair and a gray furry dog bed for

Chloe. Also meant I could watch *My Kitchen Rules* and *Married at First Sight* without Luke rubbishing the contestants every five minutes.

"Hi darling," I said poking my head through the lounge room doorway. "Had a good day?"

His eyes never left the television screen. "Mmm."

"Feel like a hot chocolate?"

"Mmm." Body language saying leave me alone, can't you see I'm watching the game, he leaned closer to the goggle-box. "Are you blind, Ump?" he shouted at the large 65" screen. "Where's Jonas's free kick? Put ya money on the other team, did ya?"

I left him to it and wandered into the kitchen. Maybe I should leave my accusations until tomorrow, when he was in a better mood. I tossed my bags on the kitchen counter where bread crumbs, an open vegemite jar and a packet of cheese lay beside a dirty knife and grabbed two clean mugs from the dishwasher. My hands shook as I made the hot chocolates and added sugar to mine and I could feel my breath catching in my throat, my chest clogging up with nerves.

Why was I getting cold feet?

I wasn't the one in the wrong, here.

And then Nathan Forrester's words pinged across my brain in flashing neon lights: *You deserve better than that, Abigail Truelove.* And he was right. I did. No more dithering, I had to know the truth. Leaving the hot chocolates where they were, sitting on the kitchen table, I headed back into the lounge.

Luke had turned the television up higher, probably to discourage conversation. So, taking a deep breath, I strode across the room, bent down, and yanked the plug out of the wall socket.

"Hey! What the hell are you doing, woman?"

I took a deep breath and before I could change my mind, swung around and faced him. "Luke, have you been having sex with Petra Sullivan?"

I could tell before he even spoke that he was guilty. His eyes had that deer in the headlights look about them.

"Abi, I think it's time we had a talk."

Oh. God. No. I closed my eyes. He wasn't even going to deny it. Wasn't even going to pretend that it was a one-off-thing and all Petra's fault. I could tell by Luke's body-language our relationship was in the gutter.

"Talk? What's there to talk about? If you cheated on me, we're finished."

He ran his fingers through his mop of dirty-blonde hair. "I should have told you a couple of months ago, when it first started."

"A couple of months ago? You and Petra have been going at it for two months?" I reeled backwards.

"Um…off and on. Look, I'm sorry, Abi. I didn't mean to hurt you. That's why it's taken this long for me to come clean."

"But Luke, you *didn't* come clean. I found out at the dog show. At the same time as thirty or forty other people who were within hearing distance."

"I'm sorry."

"Do you know how many other men Petra's slept with during those two months?"

"None. Petra might flirt a little, but she promised if I leave you, we'll have a monogamous relationship."

"Jesus, Luke, she had it off with the show judge over the weekend, just so she could win a Best in Show trophy."

"You're wrong. Petra's not like that. She's really quite sweet."

"Yeah, sweet, like a boa-constrictor." And then it hit me. "Oh, God. You've got yourself into trouble betting on the football results, haven't you?"

"What are you talking about?"

"You think, because Petra's parents are loaded, she'll help you out." I let out a forced laugh. "If so, you're delusional. Petra Sullivan looks after one person only. Herself."

"I'm not attracted to Petra because of her money," he said, and I watched him blink and chew on his bottom lip. "I love her."

Yep. His lie-detector was signaling loud and clear.

"Get out, Luke!" I scooped his jacket up from the floor where he'd dropped it and threw it at him. "Come back tomorrow while I'm at work and collect the rest of your stuff. If it's not out by then, I'll bag it and donate it to charity. I don't want to ever see your face again."

He shoved his arms through the sleeves of his jacket, sighed, and shaking his head, strode toward the door.

"And make sure you put the front door key on the kitchen table before you leave tomorrow."

He stopped and turned back. "But–"

"Get out!" I grabbed a dachshund statue from the top of the television, drew my arm back ready to aim it at his head, but at the last moment, realized the statue was more valuable than his head and put it down again. A framed photo of one of his football heroes sat beside it. I threw that instead. Smiled when the photo hit the floor and the glass cracked.

"Abi can't we–"

"And if you're having trouble finding Petra tonight, check out *The Pussycat Parlor*. You'll find your new cash-cow there, pole-dancing in front of hundreds of sweaty, drooling men."

"Whaat?" If his mouth opened any wider, I'd mistake it for a vase and start arranging flowers. "But Petra said she worked in the Food Services industry."

"She certainly works in the 'Services' industry, but I doubt there'd be much food on the menu."

"You're a liar. My little flower wouldn't show off her assets to anyone but me." His voice changed, turned into a snarl. "She knows better."

A chill ran up my spine. What would have happened if the boot had been on the other foot and I'd been the one cheating on Luke?

I wrapped my arms around my upper body and subdued a shiver as Luke slammed the door behind him.

Did I really know the man I'd been living with for the past eighteen months?

5

For the second time that night, I parked my van over the road from *The Pussy Cat Parlor*. Nerves jangling like demented church bells, I glared across at the dancing lights of the nightclub. Illumination in the shape of a female stripper, complete with cat's whiskers, little pointy ears and a bouncy tail.

After seeing Luke off the premises, I'd decided there was no way I could sleep without first telling Petra exactly what I thought of her – that she was a crooked, low-rent, boyfriend-stealing slut.

After which I'd sneak a decomposed fish into her handbag.

Yep, I'd discovered the beautiful smelly critter while delving into the Fishmonger's garbage bins. It was the one that made my eyes water the most.

Okay, I had a plan, of sorts. I knew it was no good crashing through the front door of the club, both barrels blazing, and expect to tackle Petra. I'd never get past the pole-dancer's entourage. No, I'd make my entrance through the back door. First, I'd find Petra's dressing-room (surely as the club's star attraction she'd have her name on the door) and if my nemesis was in there, I'd confront her. If not, after popping the dead fish into Petra's handbag, a handbag I knew cost her more than a return flight to New Zealand, business class, I'd make myself comfortable and wait until *enemy-number-one* came prancing through the dressing-room door. And then I'd let her have it. A full-on spray, complete with the F bomb and several other negative connotations.

Not give her a chance to get a word in edgeways.

Careful not to let the decomposing fish disintegrate, I prodded it gently into a plastic carry-bag, then swung out of the van and locked both doors. No good tempting fate in this neighborhood.

I could see Boris the bouncer/doorman leaning against the front door jamb, checking his phone. Although the noise was still deafening inside, the street in front of the club was near-empty.

Flicking the hood of my jacket up over my head, I carefully studied the area surrounding the club. There was only Boris, who was still glued to his phone – probably placing a bet on some race in Hong Kong or watching a show on iView. Someone dressed in a long black overcoat taking their dog for a walk before bedtime. And two alcohol-fueled women, dressed in flashy attire climbing noisily into a cab. Going by the conversation, their night disappointingly unproductive.

Earlier, I'd noticed an alleyway running along the back of the nightclub and figured that's where I'd find a less monitored entrance. So, wrapping the sides of my hood even further around my face, I strolled along the footpath opposite the club. Ever so nonchalantly. Just an insomniac night-owl out for a walk.

From a couple of streets away, I could hear the rhythmic chugging of a tugboat as it plowed its way along the Port river, towing a much larger boat into the safety of the wharf. The pungent reek of diesel added to the familiar river smells.

On reaching the corner and while Boris was still engrossed by the entertainment on his cell phone, I darted across the road, slipped around the side of the building and plastered my back against the wall, heart racing.

Didn't want to be spotted and questioned before I'd even found my way inside.

The night seemed darker off the main street. Lonelier. More dangerous. No bright flashing lights here, only one feeble streetlight half-heartedly attempting to illuminate a three-foot area. The others probably had their orbs smashed by stone-throwing kids at some stage and hadn't been replaced. Guess the despairing council had already installed replacement globes at least a dozen times and finally gave up.

The alleyway at the rear of the building was also badly lit. Typical. Why waste money on lighting for staff-members when the establishment's only concern was the paying public? A little creeped-out by the shadows, I peered into the semi-darkness and licked my dry lips. Maybe fronting up to Petra tonight wasn't such a good idea. There was always tomorrow to inflict a tongue lashing – in the bright light of day.

And then I thought of Petra's smirk while hinting of her sexual exploits with Luke. The way Luke defended the evil witch. Plus, the awesome *gift* I was carrying in the plastic bag. No, I had to see it through. The fish would be nothing but malodorous mush by the following day.

Gritting my teeth, I switched on my phone light.

In front of me lay a stretch of rough concrete with a drain running down the center. There were mountains of boxes haphazardly lined up against the back wall, a couple of overflowing dumpsters and crates of empty bottles stacked on top of each other. Realizing I'd stopped breathing, I quickly inhaled. Only to be overpowered by the stale smell of alcohol and urine permeating the area. In fact, this was a typical alleyway to be found at the rear of many old buildings in the Port.

Typical, but not an ideal spot for a lone woman to be hanging out at one o-clock in the morning.

A scrabbling sound behind one of the crates sent my heart leaping so high it collided with my tonsils. Hand shaking, I shone my torch in the direction of the noise and was immediately rewarded by the sight of four bright eyes.

Rats!

Oh God, if there were two rats in the alley there was probably an extended family of them hiding behind the crates and scuttling around in the nearby dumpster. And if I knew anything about rats, they were playing a game of let's-scare-the-skinny-woman-in-the-black-hoodie and then laugh as she choked to death on her screams.

Aargh…the *balls* I'd reluctantly grown at the entrance to the alleyway gave a tiny baby-squeak, threw up their hands in surrender and then went limp and floppy.

Ahead, I could see a dim light hovering over an open doorway with a large cat statue each side and a sign that read Staff Entrance.

I decided to push on.

Switching off my torch so I couldn't see any rats' eyes, I made a dash toward the safety of the doorway. Once I'd given Petra a serve, I'd exit through the front of the club, return to the safety of my car and burn rubber.

In my haste to reach the doorway before the rats ganged up on me, I almost did a face plant into the concrete by tripping over what looked like someone asleep on the ground. I cursed and grabbed at my back where it felt like I'd pulled a muscle in my attempt to stay upright. Maybe it was the drunk we'd seen earlier in the night scrambling for his dropped chips. Maybe he'd passed out or decided to sleep it off at the back of the club.

Ready to nudge him awake with the toe of my boot, I switched on my phone-torch again, and directed the beam onto the ground.

Oh, my God. My heart gave two startled beeps then came to an abrupt halt. My stomach, already heaving, plunged to my toes. I opened my mouth, tried to scream, but my breath caught in my throat and went nowhere.

It wasn't a sleeping drunk…

It was Petra Sullivan.

She was lying sprawled on her back, face the color of a ripe plum, a leather dog-lead knotted tightly around her neck.

And I didn't need to feel her pulse to know my nemesis wasn't going to cheat on anyone's boyfriend, ever again.

6

After dialing 000 and informing the police I'd found a dead body at the rear of The Pussycat Parlor, I shoved my cell into the back pocket of my trackies and stared into the semi-darkness of the laneway. A shiver ran up my spine and icy prickles caused the hairs on the back of my neck to slowly rise. I pulled my jacket more closely around my body. Suddenly it wasn't just the four-legged rats I had to be wary of, what if the two-legged rat who killed Petra was still hanging around? What if he was watching me right now? Watching and planning to use another of his deadly dog leads for a purpose it was never intended?

Suddenly rattled, I made a dash for the back door of the club, letting the door slam behind me as I careered inside and hijacked the first person I bumped into. It was a flamboyant stripper who came complete with lurid eye make-up, black painted fingernails that would have been the envy of any big-cat, and an outrageously ostentatious silk dressing gown that I guessed covered little more than a thong. The name, *Pussy Willow,* was embroidered on the front.

"Come, quick!" I wheezed, each word getting hooked on the lump in my throat. "Th-there's a dead body in the alleyway and maybe the killer is still out there."

Pussy Willow, or Sharon, as she told me to call her, switched on the main light that lit up the back alley and, grabbing one of the colorful umbrellas lined up at the back door for a weapon, followed me outside.

"Oh, my God, it's *Pussy Love*," Sharon whispered, barely getting the words out as she stared down at the body.

I frowned. "*Pussy Love*?"

"That's Petra's stage-name."

She continued to stare at the body for what felt like an eternity, but was probably only twenty seconds, before finally kneeling to check her pulse and concede that, yes, Petra was gone.

Finally, she stood up, and knuckles white as she clutched her umbrella, eyed me with suspicion. "You didn't say what *you* were doing out here in the alleyway when you found Petra's body?"

Good question. And a question I knew would be the first one asked by the police when they arrived.

What the heck had I been thinking – or in this case *not* thinking – when I decided to jump in the car and confront Petra in a nightclub, at one o'clock in the morning, via a back alleyway?

"It's sorta complicated," I said and drew in a breath trying to come up with the right words to explain what had happened. "You see, Petra cheated on me with my boyfriend so I decided to bring her a present."

Sharon blinked and her long lashes brushed against her cheek. "Why the blazes would you do that?"

I opened the top of the plastic Woolworths bag and thrust it under Sharon's nose."

First, she gagged on the nose-curling smell, and then her laugh rang out all the way down the alleyway. "Oh, God, I love it. You brought the Man-Eater a rotten fish."

"To sneak into her Gucci handbag."

"Almost wish she wasn't dead so I could see the look on her face when she opened the bag."

I tipped my head to the side and studied my new friend. "You don't seem very upset about Petra's death."

"Why should I be? Petra's no friend of mine. In fact, now she's gone, I get to be star pole-dancer. Plus, one of my best mates committed suicide because of her. She led him on then dumped him very publicly.

Poor guy threw himself in front of a train." She shrugged one shoulder. All nonchalant. "Doesn't mean I killed her though."

I blinked. People had killed for far less. "What about the other workers at the club? Can you think of anyone who hated Petra enough to murder her?"

"Everyone, I guess. Petra wasn't what you call BFF material." She shifted her chewing gum from one side of her mouth to the other, studying the body, head tipped to the side. "You know, that isn't just any old dog leash. Petra's been strangled with a *Chanel* dog leash. I know, because I bought a collar and lead set just like it for my Pomeranian, Mimi. Cost me almost half of what I paid for these shoes." She lifted one foot to show-off an elegant gold-colored high-heeled Valentino sandal. "Nothing's too good for my darling Mimi."

I bent to check the murder weapon more closely. Sharon was right. Petra had been strangled with a designer dog-leash, one that I stocked at my pet boutique *Pampered Pooch* for one hundred and fifty dollars, three hundred if it included the matching bespoke leather collar.

I'd been so shaken on finding the body, the actual panache of the murder weapon hadn't registered.

I slowly got to my feet. Did this mean the murderer was from the show-dog world? Someone I knew? I shivered. Had I *sold* the murder weapon to Petra's killer? "You're right." I wrapped my arms around my body in a vain attempt to douse the goosebumps. "It's definitely a leash used in the show ring, or on a pampered pet. Not something you'd buy for your average backyard mutt."

Sharon didn't answer. Instead, she bent to pick up a shiny object that lay half-hidden under one of Petra's high-heeled shoes that had come off in the struggle. "What do you make of this?" She opened her hand. A gold button the size of a ten-cent piece lay on her outstretched palm. "Clue, do you think?" She placed one hand on her hip and tipped her head back in a sultry pose. "Reckon I'd make a good Phryne Fisher?"

I let out a laugh at her reference to Phryne Fisher, the wealthy aristocrat and private-detective character in Australian author Kerry

Greenwood's television series, Miss Fisher's Murder Mysteries. And then a wave of guilt took my breath away. We were standing over the dead body of Petra Sullivan, a woman who'd been vitally alive and performing simulated sex on her greased-up pole only an hour ago, and now here she was dead. Life extinguished. Strangled to death with a *Chanel* dog leash.

"You'd better put that button back where you found it. Police won't be happy if they discover you've tampered with the crime scene."

Sharon lifted one heavily-made-up eyebrow and grinned. "Can't do that, can I? My fingerprints are on the button now."

"Hmm…maybe you'd better drop the button in my pocket then." I ran my eyes over the stripper's lurid silk dressing gown, which was now gaping open at the front, revealing, as I'd imagined, nothing but a thong and a few splatters of gold paint. "'Cos *you* don't seem to have anywhere safe to stash it."

Sharon shoved the button into my hand. "Here. Petra will need all the help she can get, 'cos I don't trust the cops to take a pole-dancer's death too seriously. *Pussy Galore*, one of our part-time strippers, was beaten up by some guy a month ago and the cops barely raised an eye brow when she reported it." Her jaw set as she frowned at me. "*Pussy Love*, alias Petra Sullivan, might have been the Queen of sluts, but she still deserves justice." She grabbed my hand and squeezed. "Find out who owns that button, okay?"

"Do my best." I squeezed Sharon's hand in return then examined the button. It was gold with small intricate circles around the edge, quite distinctive. "It's likely this came off the killer's jacket while Petra was fighting for her life."

"Yeah, that's what *I'm* thinking."

"Okay, leave it with me." Firstly, I took a quick photo of the evidence then slipped the button into the bag with the fish, reasoning that not even the most diligent policeman would want to poke around in there.

"Hey, what's going on?"

We both jumped as the back door flew open with a crash and a belligerent voice bellowed out into the alleyway. A hulk of a guy with a crew-cut and an attitude that could tame wild bears came charging through the doorway.

"H-hey, Spence." Sharon drew her dressing gown more tightly around her body and took a step back before answering his question. "Looks like *Pussy Love* might have slept with the wrong guy this time. Someone's gone and strangled her. She's dead."

"Dead? Christ! The boss's gonna be pissed big time when he hears about this." Bull-like face contorted into an aggravated snarl, he strode toward us, his heavy boots attacking the ground at every stride. "Why the hell couldn't the bitch have got herself offed some other place? Why here? Now we'll have the blasted cops nosing around, askin' questions and stickin' their snouts into what don't concern 'em."

I frowned. *And finding what? More dead bodies? Money-laundering? Drugs?*

He came to a stop beside Petra's body, squatted down to feel for a pulse, then, with another eye-watering expletive, tossed her arm back on the ground like a piece of garbage.

Even in my warm hooded jacket, I shivered at Spence's callousness. The moment I'd come across Petra's body, my own animosity had vanished. Petra looked so vulnerable splayed out on the ground, her near-naked body exposed to the dark uncaring sky. Wide staring eyes that would never see another sunrise. And I could tell by the way Petra's gold-painted fingernails were jagged and broken that she'd put up one hell of a fight. It looked to me as though the killer had come from behind, surprised his victim, and then wrapped the dog leash around her neck. And as Petra fought to free herself, the killer had wrenched the leash tighter and tighter around her throat, until she'd finally choked out her last gasping breath.

"Righto, listen up, this's what's gonna happen." Spence, having finished examining the body was now fully into damage-control. "I'll get Bruno to reverse one of our vans into the alley, we'll sling Petra's body in the back and then he can drive over to her place and dump her in the gutter outside. That way, the cops'll go nosing around on the other side of town, instead of here." He dragged out his two-way radio, clicked to activate it and then lifted one bushy eyebrow at us. "And best of all, the boss won't go apeshit and start shooting out kneecaps."

"Um…" *Shooting our kneecaps?* I gave a small cough. When that didn't catch Spence's attention I tried again, a little louder. "Um…that's sort of not an option, I'm afraid. See, I-I've already contacted the police." I gritted my teeth and flinched, half-expecting to feel a hard fist slam into my face. "A-and they know I found Petra's body here, in the laneway."

Spence glanced up from his two-way radio and his hard eyes bored into mine. "And who the hell are you?"

"Abigail Truelove. I found Petra's body."

He shoved his two-way back into his pocket and spat on the ground so close to my feet that my left sneaker caught the overflow. "And you rang the cops?"

"Sorry."

"Well, Abigail Truelove, you've caused us all a great deal of trouble." He stepped closer, towering over me by close to a foot. "And the boss and I, we don't like trouble, see." Teeth clenched in a snarl, he leaned forward and pushed his face close to mine, the garlic he'd consumed earlier in the night making my eyes water.

I took a step backward, body tensed, poised for flight. Geez, what a night! Not only had I broken up with Luke and tripped over the dead body of his new girlfriend, now I was bailed up in a back alley with a garlic-eating gorilla, who, if 'the boss' instructed him to, would not only shoot out my kneecaps he'd probably snap my neck like a twig and toss my body into the nearby dumpster. And by the way Spence was eyeballing me right now, I wasn't sure he'd wait for instructions.

"Come on, Abi." Sharon hooked me by the sleeve of my jacket, subtly maneuvering me away from Spence. "We're freezing our arse off out here. Let's go wait for the fuzz in my dressing room. Reckon we could both do with a snifter of brandy. It's not every night you find a dead body."

"But I can't leave the scene of the crime. The police will want to question me."

One eye on Spence, Sharon pulled harder on my sleeve. "Don't worry, a cop's nose is trained to sniff out *a toke in a rubbish dump*, so doesn't matter where you are, they'll find you."

Ten minutes later, the blare of police sirens invaded my overstuffed brain as I perched on a fluffy stool inside Sharon's dressing-room, a stiff brandy in one hand the Woolworths bag containing the decomposed fish on the floor at my feet. My thoughts were running amok in my brain like delinquent children. What was I doing here? How did I get myself involved in this mess? Would the police shred what little brain I had left with a barrage of unanswerable questions?

Hey, all I'd wanted to do was give Petra a verbal blast and then stink up her favorite *Gucci* handbag.

Suddenly, without warning, I felt bone weary. I could barely keep from resting my head amongst the make-up and beauty products scattered all over *Pussy Willow's* dressing-table. I wanted to go home, curl up on my crisp pale blue sheets and snuggle under my new quilt, the one featuring frolicking dachshunds in all their mischievous moods. I'd bought the quilt from *Pampered Pooch* when the shipment first arrived two weeks ago.

Before I'd found out that Paul had cheated on me.

Before Petra had been murdered.

Before my own life turned into a bag of rotting fish.

I let out a sigh, gulped down the last of my brandy, false courage, and turned to ask Sharon for a refill.

That's when a plain-clothes detective and three uniforms shouldered their way through the dressing-room door.

"Hey, didn't your mothers ever teach you lot to knock?" Sharon, minuscule thong and gold paint on full display, let out a squeak of surprise before snatching up the robe she'd only minutes ago peeled off. She drew the robe back on again while the three uniforms, eyes struggling not to take a peek at her goodies, fanned out across the room.

The suit, all stony-faced authority and stick up his rear, zeroed in on me. "I'm Detective Lightfoot, the officer in charge." He held his warrant card up for me to peruse. "And you are?"

"Abigail Truelove." I upended my glass to suck up the dregs clinging to the bottom, then eyed the half-full bottle of brandy on Sharon's dressing-table with longing.

"Are you the person who found the deceased?"

Deceased? I swallowed the dry lump in my throat. "The *deceased* might have been a two-bit cheating slut, but she did have a name, you know. It's Petra Sullivan."

"Or *Pussy Love,* as she's known here, at The Pussycat Parlor," Sharon butted in, lips pouting.

Detective Stick-Up-His-Rear flicked his icy-blue orbs across to rest on Sharon. "And you are?"

"*Pussy Willow.*" When he lifted one bushy eyebrow and continued to stare, she sighed. "Okay, I'm Sharon Bottomley."

"And did you find the body, Ms. Bottomley?"

"No, but–"

"Well, please refrain from answering questions not directed at you." He switched his minus 50-degree stare back onto me. "I'll repeat the question, Ms. Truelove. Did you find the deceased in the alley?"

"Yes. In fact, I tripped over her. Almost put my back out."

He looked me up and down, his uncomplimentary nose-curl indicating he was not impressed by my comfortable runners, tatty black track-pants and out-of-shape hoodie. "Judging by your attire, I doubt you were a patron of the club tonight, so, what exactly were you doing in the alleyway at the back of The Pussycat Parlor at this time of the morning?"

I sucked in a deep breath as though it was my last. In fact, it might be as I really didn't have a good answer to that question. "Um, well, I came here to see Petra and thought I'd have a better chance of catching her if I used the back entrance."

"Ah, so you admit you were here to see the deceased?"

"Yes, to *see* her, but not to *kill* her." I sucked in another breath. Strange how attempting to prove you're not a murderer made breathing so difficult. "Okay, I admit I was angry with Petra. Why wouldn't I be? She slept with my boyfriend and caused us to break up, so I came here to yell at her, tell her exactly what I thought of her."

His eyes narrowed. "Instead, you found her body?"

"Yeah, okay, but geez, all I wanted to do was give her a mouthful, and then, maybe, slip a present into her *Gucci* handbag."

"A present?"

"A rotten fish."

The corner of his lips quirked upwards, ever so slightly, and just as quickly flattened again. He pointed to the Woolworths' bag at my feet. "Judging by the stench emanating from in there, I'm guessing that's your present?"

Before I could answer, he snatched up the bag and instead of peering inside, he upended the contents onto the dressing-room floor.

The decomposing fish fell apart on impact, the smell had everyone gagging, and a gold button, the size of a ten-cent piece, rolled slowly across the floor and came to rest at Detective Lightfoot's feet.

It might have been Sharon's guilty gasp or the fact that I hastily reached for the brandy, chugging straight from the bottle, but Detective Lightfoot's jaw hardened into a solid concrete block and his eyes narrowed to slits. He scooped up the button, studied it like it was the Holy Grail and then drilled me with his icy blues.

"Does this belong to you, Ms. Truelove?"

"Noo." I dragged the word out, hoping it would give me time to think of a reasonable excuse for the button to be shaking hands with my rotten fish. Didn't work. I couldn't think of a damn thing – other than the truth. "Um…it was in the alley, near the body."

"And you removed it?" He paused between each word. His voice icier than the wind in a snowstorm. "You *do* know that tampering with a crime scene and concealing evidence is an indictable offence?"

"Well…"

"It wasn't her. Abi didn't find the button. I did." Sharon jumped to her feet her garishly made-up eyes sending me a silent message, which I deciphered as *'keep quiet, leave this to me'*. "*I found the button beside Petra's body. Abi was merely looking after it for me.*"

"Why?" Detective Lightfoot stepped into the stripper's personal space. "Did you lose the button when you killed *Pussy Love*? Did it get ripped off your dressing-gown while you struggled with the deceased? Is that why you asked Ms. Truelove to hide the evidence?"

Sharon's laugh resonated in the room like an empty shipping container. She didn't back away, instead she stepped closer, her gold-painted boobs, uncovered when her gown fell apart in her agitation, an inch away from the detective's jacket. "You're way off base, copper. You want to know why I kept the evidence? It's because you lot won't spend more than five minutes tracking down the owner of that button. *Pussy Love* was a stripper, working in a nightclub. To you lot, she's trash, not someone you'd put yourselves out for. Just ask *Pussy Galore* who got beaten up by a customer last month. What did you do for her? Exactly nothing, that's what."

"Ms. Bottomley, you didn't answer my question." Detective Lightfoot's voice gave a slight hitch. He stepped away from the boob-attack, his face bright red, probably from trying hard not to let his eyes drop below the level of her face. "Did you hide the evidence because you killed the deceased?"

"Of course not. Okay, Petra Sullivan wasn't what you'd call a nice person, but she was a colleague, so, rather than leave the investigation to the police, I decided to track down the owner of the gold button myself. I had nowhere safe to hide it so I dropped it in with Abi's fish. Okay?"

Evidently it wasn't okay. Because after that, the interview slid downhill faster than shares in a stock-market crash, ending with Sharon being led away in handcuffs.

"Abi," she called out as two of the officers escorted her to the door.

"Can you look after Mimi for me until I get out?"

Her dog? "Um…no problem. Where is she?"

"Unit 8, 25 Foxglove Drive, Port Adelaide." With a nod of her head she indicated a set of keys lying amongst the scattered make-up on the dressing-table. "And don't forget your promise."

Find out who owns the missing button…

Difficult, as the evidence was now in a plastic baggie deep inside one of Detective Lightfoot's pockets. So, wasn't it lucky I had a photo of the gold button with the intricate edging tucked away in the 'picture gallery' on my cell phone?

"Don't worry, Sharon. I'll do what I can."

Detective Lightfoot shot me a glare loaded with snake venom. "I still haven't finished with you, Ms. Truelove, so don't poke your nose into our investigation and don't leave town. Otherwise, you could find yourself locked up in the same cell as your friend."

7

Nine hours later, I could feel myself going all gooey as I watched my little wiener dog, Chloe, perform a series of Pepe la Pew leaps on her stumpy little legs, while making her way across the polished wooden floor of my lounge room.

Ears flapping, eyes brimming with mischief, she carried her favorite green and yellow squeaky ball in her mouth as she challenged Penelope to catch her. Not easy, as Chloe could squeeze her entire sausage-like body under the sofa whereas Penelope was lucky to even fit her long greyhound snout underneath.

My extraverted dachshund absolutely adored it when Busta or Penelope came for a visit. Today, she was over the moon. She had a new friend to play with as well.

Sharon's little princess, Mimi.

Problem was – Mimi wasn't interested in joining in Chloe's games. Still wearing the pajamas I'd found her in–featuring miniscule Pooh Bears on a sunset yellow background–Mimi was too busy sulking in the corner of my lounge room and growling at every human or canine that came within two feet of her royal presence.

After being dismissed by Detective Lightfoot around 3 that morning, I'd returned to my car. But while programming my van's GPS satnav to direct me to Sharon's house to collect Mimi, the front door of *The Pussycat Parlor* shot open. Two policemen, expressions neutral, strode out carrying a stretcher. I watched as they transferred Petra's bagged-up body into a silent ambulance. At the time, none of it seemed real. In fact, I almost expected Petra to rip open the bag, leap off the stretcher and start complaining to everyone in earshot about the lucrative tips she was missing out on by being dead.

Why was a young woman so alive and vibrant while performing in the club less than three hours earlier, now dead? Had she pushed some guy's buttons and he'd snapped? Videoed a secret rendezvous with some paranoid celebrity and then blackmailed him by threatening to upload the video to Social Media and make sure it went viral? Or had she slept with a guy who got his kicks out of choking his bed companion – and this time he'd gone too far?

Tired, disillusioned and still shaking, I'd driven to Foxglove Road and found unit 8 tucked away in a little cul-de-sac, in a rather upmarket part of Port Adelaide. But that was the easy part. Persuading the diminutive, but rather grumpy, Mimi, to come home with me without turning my fingers into chopped liver, had proven quite a bit harder.

I'd found her curled up asleep inside a satin-lined shoe box beside Sharon's bed. The little dog looked so cute and so sweet dressed in her flannel pajamas. However, as soon as those dark brown eyes opened and zeroed in on me, both cuteness and sweetness took off on a ten-mile hike.

One look at me and Mimi had exploded into a volley of barking and pure annihilation. More hair than dog, and a front end with the fire power of a Glock 22, Sharon's little Princess left a set of teeth marks on my right wrist that went almost to the bone. And it would have been a lot worse, if I hadn't smothered the beast in a doggy-blanket so I could shove her into her crate, and quickly deposit crate and dog onto the passenger seat of the van.

Breed – Pomeranian.

Temperament – Sister of Satan.

And ever since I'd brought her home, the hyped-up Pom had done nothing but sulk, snarl, and snap.

"What's with the urgent text to meet you here at noon?" Dana, who was kneeling on the floor changing Jake's diaper, broke into my thoughts. "Sounds, ominous."

"It is. There's something important I need to tell you and Molly." I let out a sigh. After three hours spent tossing and turning instead of sleeping, followed by a busy morning serving customers at *Pampered Pooch*, I'd rather be curled up in bed right now, catching up on lost shut-eye. But, with Petra's murder looming over my head, I needed the support of my friends even more. "Look, I know we discussed maybe resurrecting *The Gumshoe Chicks* last night, but I could really do with your help. Big time. Veronique, my oh-so-reliable assistant, is in charge of the shop, so I thought it would be a good time to get us all together."

"If it's about Petra's murder, I heard it on the early-morning news. And I don't see why *we* need to investigate. It's an open and shut case. She slept with the wrong guy and got herself whacked." Dana lifted Jake up and set him down on the floor where he immediately toddled over to the sofa, lay on his stomach, reached underneath and took Chloe's squeaky ball out of her mouth. He then pushed himself back onto his feet, toddled over to Mimi and presented the now-soggy ball to her. Satan's Little Sister wagged her tail, licked the little boy's face and ran off in the direction of the kitchen with the ball in her mouth, hotly pursued by both Chloe and Penelope.

Well done, Jake.

After exchanging a conspirator's grin, Dana straightened up to her full height of 5' 9". That's in flats. She could look in most guy's eyes when she wore heels. "What about Luke?" she said and sniffed, as though a rotten egg had dropped out of the sky. "Did you rip strips off his cheating backside before you threw him out the door?"

"Got a direct hit with one of his footy pictures, which broke on impact."

"Good." Dana's face softened and she threw an arm around my shoulders. "And are *you* okay now that he's gone?"

Was I okay? I sent Dana a wobbly grin. "You know, I think I am. He was never there for me. And after the first few months of our relationship, I was nothing more than his cleaner, cook and backside wiper. In a way, Petra did me a favor."

"That witch did no one any favors, but I know what you mean." Alerted by the muffled sound of Jake's giggling, Dana poked her head around the kitchen doorway to check on the cause of the mirth. She rolled her eyes, before relieving Jake of the iced donut he was feeding the dogs and replacing it with several doggy treats she dug out of her pocket. "Now," she said turning back to me, all business. "What's this meeting really about?"

"Can we wait for Molly?" I gave Dana my best doe-eye. "Otherwise, I'll have to tell the story twice."

Dana dropped Jake's wet nappy, encased in a plastic bag, into the kitchen litterbin and rinsed her hands under the tap over the sink. "In that case, you can start clearing your throat in readiness, 'cos Molly just pulled up outside. I can tell by the putt-putt of her little toy car." She ripped a sheet of kitchen-towel from the roll and wiped her hands, before screwing it up and dropping it in the bin. "I don't know how she manages to get from A to B in that contraption. Keep telling her it's time she bought something with a bit more grunt."

There was a knock on the door.

I placed another bowl of cheese and onion crisps on the kitchen table, next to a king-sized box of gourmet donuts I'd picked up from the bakery, before calling out. "Hey, Moll, come on in. Door's open."

As Molly trundled through the doorway, she bent to unhook Busta's leash, so he could join in the game of ball that had now moved back into the lounge room. "This better be good," she grumbled as she made her way into the kitchen. "My besotted protagonists, Sebastian and Rebecca, were mid-plunge and steaming up all the windows, and I was just getting to the good part where he tells her he has to return to Ireland and wants her to go with him, and she can't, because her mother's ill, when your text popped onto my phone."

I grinned as one of Australia's most successful romance authors flopped onto the nearest chair. "Sorry Moll, but this is a real-life drama. Sebastian and Rebecca can wait. They're only your imaginary friends. Okay?"

Imaginary friends who paid her mortgage each month.

Once Molly and Dana were settled at the table with a glass of wine and their favorite donut squatting on a plate in front of them, I swallowed the lump in my throat and let loose with my news. "I guess you heard about Petra's murder on the television, well, I was the one who found her body."

"Body? Murder? What are you talking about?" Molly blinked at me, mouth wide open. She'd evidently been too steeped in her fictional world this morning to have listened to the news, or read a newspaper.

"Yes, Petra's been murdered."

"And *you* found her body?" Donut half-way to her mouth, Dana's face blanched. "Oh, my God. How? When? Are you okay?"

"Not really." The threatening lump was trying to work its way back up into my throat. I sniffed. Pushed the lump down again. This wasn't the time for a meltdown. I had to talk Dana and Molly into helping me get Sharon out of jail. Prove she had nothing to do with Petra's murder. "After I dropped you home last night, I broke up with Luke and–"

"Good," said Dana.

"About time," said Molly.

I blinked back a tear that lurked in the corner of my eye. Good friends like Dana and Molly were worth more than a treasure-chest full of gold bullion. "Naturally, after that, I had to return to the *Pussycat Parlor* so I could explain to Petra exactly how many brands of slut I thought she was."

Dana nodded. "Naturally."

"But you should have called us instead of going back on your own."

"It was too late by then, Moll. Anyway, thing is, when I *did* find Petra, she was dead. Strangled with a *Chanel* dog-leash." Suddenly cold, I wrapped both arms around my body. "It was awful. One look at her red bloated face and you could tell how much she'd struggled as the leash tightened around her neck."

Molly's warm hand reached across the table to squeeze mine. "What did the police have to say?"

"What *didn't* they say! The detective in charge was a guy with absolutely zero sense of humor. A total jerk. He treated me like a criminal and he took *Pussy Willow*, a stripper from the club who came out into the alley to help me, into custody. Accused her of murdering Petra. Just because she tampered with the evidence." I let out a sigh that came from somewhere near my toes. "And I'm a suspect too."

Immediately Dana's body stiffened. She scowled. "That's the most ridiculous thing I've ever heard. You're the biggest softie this side of the equator. Geez, you catch spiders in a jar and then relocate them rather than do what I do – give the blighters a taste of bug spray or a whack with a rolled-up newspaper." She grabbed my other hand and hung on.

While Molly and Dana fussed around like a couple of mother hens, filling my glass with wine and rubbing my back, I told them all about what happened in the alley and how Detective Lightfoot's last words, as my co-conspirator was taken off to jail, were, *'I haven't finished with you, Ms. Truelove, so don't leave town!'*.

"That's merely standard procedure," said Dana in a comforting, don't-you-worry voice. "*You* found the body, so naturally, he'll be wanting to speak to you again. However, before that happens, I proclaim the *Gumshoe Chicks* begin their own investigation."

"I second that," said Molly, getting to her feet and fisting the air. "Let's find out who whacked the witch and stop Detective Grumpy from threatening our Abi."

"Won't be easy," I told her while smothering a grin. *'Whacked the witch'*, sounded cute coming from Molly, the romance writer. "I could fill a notebook with the names of people who'd like to see Petra dead. Starting with almost everyone in the dog show world. Petra cheated to win in the show-ring, she slept with competitors' partners, she smirked her way through every dog show. *Plus*, she was strangled with a show leash. Pretty hot clue, I reckon."

"What about Luke?" Dana asked. "How did he react when you confronted him about sleeping with Petra? What sort of mood was he in when he left? Could he have gone to *The Pussycat Parlor*, had a fight with Petra and then strangled her?"

"I don't know. Like, he wasn't happy when he found out where Petra worked, but I think, in his own way, he loved her." I shook my head. "And anyway, this murder was premeditated. The killer brought along a dog leash for the sole purpose of using it to strangle Petra. Luke has never taken Chloe for a walk. Always insisted she was my dog therefore caring for her was my job. He had no reason to carry a dog-leash around in his pocket."

"Careful, sweetie!" Dana swept Jake, who was in the middle of a rough and tumble with the four dogs, into her arms and deposited him kicking and squealing into his playpen, where he immediately began to howl. Barely batting an eye, she upended a sack of toys she'd brought along with her into the enclosure and the noise promptly stopped. Then, task completed, she turned back to me. "What about the evidence you found near the body? What was that?"

"A button. Well, actually, it was *Pussy Willow*, from the club, who spotted the button and because she believed the police wouldn't waste their time investigating a stripper's murder, she hid the evidence in my bag. Well, in a plastic Woolworths bag containing a rather smelly dead fish. A present for Petra. Unfortunately, Detective Ice-Cubes found the button when he upended my bag, and promptly confiscated it. He also took *Pussy Willow*, or Sharon as she's really called, into custody for tampering with evidence at a crime scene." I dug my cell phone from my pocket, clicked through my Album until I brought up the photo I'd taken in the alley. "Here's a picture of the button. This is what we need to look for." I held the phone in the air. "See, it's gold and has distinctive markings around the edge."

Molly snaffled the phone and studied the photo intently. "You know, that show judge who gave Petra's pug Best in Show, he was wearing a jacket with gold buttons like that. I remember how they shone in the sun when he moved."

"I didn't notice at the show, but I thought I saw gold buttons on the jacket he wore at *The Pussycat Parlor* last night."

"Hang on," said Dana, as she skillfully retrieved her phone from the depths of her overflowing bag. "I took several photos of you two in the Best in Show line-up. Maybe Oliver T. Hutchins is in one of them." She brought up her picture gallery and quickly scrolled down until she stopped, lifted her head, and grinned. "You're right, Moll. There's six gold buttons on the judge's jacket." She began fiddling with the phone again. "Okay, this is as far as I can zoom in, but what we have here is very, very interesting."

Grinning widely, she passed the phone across to me. "If those buttons don't match the one on your phone, I'm a monkey's Aunty."

I blinked at the enlarged photo of one of the buttons on the judge's jacket and let out a whoop. "Bingo! We have lift-off!"

"So, all we have to do now is get a gander at that jacket. Check to see if there's a button missing. And if there is – we've nailed the killer."

"And, as one of the organizers of The Ladies Kennel Club show, I did all Mr. Hutchins' accommodation and flight bookings," I told them, my grin widening. "So, I know for a fact that he's booked into the *Slug and Spinach* hotel right now. I also know that he's due to return to Sydney on Qantas, flight 21 at 6.00 pm tonight."

"Woohoo!" Dana whipped Jake under her arm and folded his playpen in one swoop. "Doesn't leave us much time, though."

"So…what are we waiting for?" Molly whistled for Busta and when he came zooming out of the lounge, mouth wide, tongue hanging, she clipped on his leash. "I'll go home, collect my lock picks and meet you outside the *Slug and Spinach* in half an hour. Okay?"

Dana and I regarded Molly as though she was an alien who'd landed on the roof in a spacecraft.

"Lock picks?" Dana queried.

"Since when did you arm yourself with a burglar's toolkit?" I demanded.

"Since I lost my front door key for the third time. I got tired of locking myself out and having to ring a locksmith, so I went on YouTube, studied the art of picking locks, and invested in a set for myself. Now, I have a new front door key, *plus* a way of getting in next time the key goes astray."

Not only had Molly turned into an alien, she was bright green, had six feelers and a whizzing propeller on her head. I blinked at her. "And if you lose the lock picks?"

By now, Molly and Busta had disappeared in the direction of the front door. Her voice floated back to the kitchen. "I've hidden the picks under a most inconspicuous rock in my garden."

Dana let out a hoot and slapped one hand down on the table. "Yesss! Our sweet little Molly isn't such a soft pink marshmallow after all. She's more like one of those giant gobstopper sweets. You now, suck one and you're okay – but take a bite and you break one or more of your teeth."

My stomach did a nosedive as I recalled Petra's bloodied broken front teeth. Not from a gobstopper – but from a fist to the face. Probably to stop her struggling.

8

"You're late." Molly, wearing a long black overcoat, her dark hair swinging across her pale face, greeted us in the parking lot of the *Slug and Spinach*. I stifled a grin. If Disney ever decided to turn one of those paranormal cozy mysteries – now popular with readers – into a movie, Molly would be a shoo-in to play the part of the witchy protagonist.

"Sorry," I called out through the open window as Dana parked her SUV beside Molly's lovingly restored red 1963 Morris Mini Cooper. "We were almost ready to leave when Jake discovered a large jar of vegemite in my kitchen pantry. Had to smear it all over himself, didn't he? Put me off having kids for life."

The *Slug and Spinach,* an English-themed pub that came complete with a Union Jack plastered across the front entrance, was set well back off the street and utilized a shady, well-treed car park out front.

"Well, at least one of us has been investigating." Molly, who looked like the cat that ate the kippers and was now cleaning its whiskers, hitched her tote-bag higher onto her shoulder. "While you two were de-vegemite-ing Jake, which, although sounds exceedingly gross, would have to be easier than de-honeying or de-treacle-ing him, *I've* been poking around inside the pub. *And* I found our target." She gave an exaggerated toss of her head. "Oliver T. Hutchins is currently draped across one of the lounges in the foyer, nose deep in a newspaper."

While Dana gave Penelope, the greyhound, a liver treat before unstrapping Jake from his baby capsule in the back seat of her car, I joined Molly, eager to hear more. "Well, let's hear it. Is he by himself? Does he look guilty? Is he wearing the jacket with the gold buttons?"

"Hey, down, girl!" Molly put two hands, palms up, in front of her and shook her head at me. "He's by himself. He looks neither guilty nor innocent. And he's dressed casually, in grey slacks and a blue and white striped shirt." Still thinking, she wrinkled her forehead, which on Molly always looked more cute, than contemplative. "Although…" She dragged the word out. "He *does* appear a little on edge. Keeps glancing up from his paper to check people walking past."

"Could be he just enjoys people-watching. I always do when I'm out and about on my own."

"Or, maybe he's worried the police are going to nab him before he can board the plane and disappear." Dana, with a wriggling Jake now strapped into his stroller, trundled up beside them while Molly was talking. She dug deep into her bottomless purse and extracted a scruffy vomit-yellow plush toy dog which she handed to her irascible son. Immediately his wriggling ceased. He sent us one of his most angelic heart-melting grins. The grin that would see Jake Fox breaking hearts in the foreseeable future. He snuggled the tattered toy dog to his chest, chatting away to it in his own baby lingo while Dana zipped up her purse and turned back to Molly. "I don't suppose you learned the judge's room number while you were nosing around inside the pub?"

"As a matter of fact, I did." Molly gave a smirk and shrugged one shoulder as if to say, *'Isn't that what all good investigators do?'*

"Well done, Molly." I punched her lightly on the arm and grinned. "And here's me thinking your head would still be at home with Sebastian and Rebecca, figuring out how to save your star-struck lovers from their current dilemma."

"Well, to be honest," Molly's smirk morphed into a cheeky grin, "his room number sort-of landed in my lap. While the receptionist was busy answering the phones, I strolled across to the main desk, and there, for all to see, was the hotel register. And guess what? It was wide open at the page displaying Mr. Oliver T. Hutchins' signature." She shook her head. "Almost like it was fate."

"And his room number is?" Dana was always the least patient of our team.

"Room number 4, which is on the first floor."

"So, before we go in, what's the plan?"

"I can use my lock picks. I'm pretty sure I remember how after studying the instructions on YouTube."

"Doubt we'll need them, Molly. Most hotels use key-cards now." I hated to burst her bubble as she was on such a high, but it had to be said. Molly, being so sweet, and such a great listener, was our best choice to keep Hutchins talking, while Dana and I slipped upstairs and tried to convince a cleaner to let us into room 4.

"But I want to be in on the action too," Molly protested once I outlined my plan and Dana approved.

"You're our key player," Dana told her. "It will be up to you to keep our suspect downstairs in the foyer. If he catches us in his room, we'll be in deep doo-doo. Probably in a police van hightailing it to the nearest police station." Dana leaned in and spoke slowly, persuasively. "Molly, if anyone can get our suspect talking, it's you. You have the gift. Geez, you can start a conversation with anyone, from a celebrity to a homeless guy. Don't know how you do it."

"But what if you do need my lock picks?" You can say one thing about Molly – she didn't give up easily.

"We'll shoot you a text. Okay?"

Once through the hotel's automatic front doors, I could see Hutchins splayed on a nearby lounge chair, his nose in this morning's *Advertiser*. He glanced up, frowned, as though he sort-of recognized our faces, but couldn't quite remember from where, then his concentration went back to his paper.

"Go on, Molly," Dana ordered, giving her an unsubtle push in the back. "Go do your thing!"

"B-but what'll I talk about?"

"Anything!" said Dana.

"Dogs," I suggested. "He's a judge. You're a competitor. Introduce yourself. Tell him you showed under him on the weekend and ask his advice about some problem you have with Busta. Judges love to ramble on about how much knowledge they have."

Molly screwed up her nose. "But I don't have a problem with Busta."

"Make. One. Up." Dana growled through gritted teeth. And with that, she bolted toward the lifts with Jake happily babbling away to his vomit-yellow dog and lifting the toy up to show every person they passed.

I caught up with them seconds before the lift doors clanged shut.

"Hang on, Dana," I growled as I forced the doors apart and scrambled into the escalator. "Hotel's not on fire."

"Maybe not, but we don't know how long Molly can keep Hutchins talking. She's a fabulous listener. Has all the necessary eye and mouth expressions down to a fine art. But she's not what you'd call a great ad-libber, is she?"

I nodded. Dana was right. Molly could get *anyone* talking – even a shy introvert – but she wasn't one for contributing a hell of a lot to the conversation, except eye-contact, beatific smiles and focused attentiveness.

"And if he loses interest, he could come stomping back to his room ready to pack." Dana went on. "Which means we have to treat this assignment as if the hotel *is* on fire. Okay?"

One floor up, the lift came to a juddering halt. I stepped out and looked around. Typical of most hotel accommodation, there was a long corridor with rooms on either side. Room number 4 was only two doors down from the lift.

I could hear faint music and laughter coming from the bar downstairs and nearby a female voice singing, the Beatles, *Yellow Submarine.* The singing seemed to be coming from inside a room halfway down the corridor. A room with a cleaner's trolley stationed outside. The trolley was piled high with sheets, towels, shampoo and conditioner samples, little soaps and rolls of toilet paper.

"Okay, here's what we'll do," said Dana as she commandeered Jake's much-loved but threadbare dog with a 'sorry sweetie, Mummy will give Doggo back soon', and quickly stuffed it into her bag. "Jake's going to start screaming any minute from now and we'll use that as an excuse to ask the nice cleaner-lady to let us into room number 4. We've misplaced our key card and the baby's over-tired and due for a feed. Right?"

I nodded and peered down at Jake. Mesmerized.

First, his eyes widened in stunned disbelief. Then his pouting bottom lip trembled, his little baby face screwed up into a crumpled red ball, and an outraged roar exploded from his mouth like a blast from a dynamite detonation. I covered my ears with both hands and cringed. Wouldn't have been surprised if the blast took out every window in the hotel.

It took no more than twenty seconds before a head popped around the open door beside the cleaner's trolley.

"Everything alright?" she shouted. Even then we could barely hear her over Jake's howling.

Jumping to attention, I began fussing around in my bag, pretending to hunt for my keycard, while Dana, putting on a frazzled face, rocked Jake's pusher.

"Damn," I said still rifling through my bag. "Where did I put that keycard?"

"Can I help?" Dressed in a pink cotton uniform with the *Slug and Spinach* emblem featured on the two front pockets, the cleaner, a red-headed woman in her early thirties came bustling towards us.

Dana let out a sigh that would have won her an Oscar on the stage. "It's been a busy morning and my little guy's overtired. Poor mite's also due for a feed." Dramatic frown in place, she turned to me. "Abi, hurry up and open the door. Any minute we'll have the hotel manager complaining about the noise."

I made my bag-rummaging actions more frantic. "I can't find our keycard! Must have left it in the glove box of the car."

"Oh no!" Dana shook the pusher harder, making Jake scream louder. "And our car's parked right over the other side of the car-park. What are we going to do? Jake will have a fit if he has to wait until you go downstairs to the car park."

"Um…would you like me to let you in now and you can collect your keycard from your car after you've settled the little man down?" The pink-clad cleaner bent to pat the kicking screaming Jake on his blonde curly head. "There, there, little dumpling. Don't cry." She came close to getting a fist in the face for her troubles.

"Oh, you're a life-saver. Jake gets so stressed when he's tired and hungry."

"No worries." Removing a communal keycard from her pocket, the cleaner quickly ran it through the device, pushed the door open and smiled at us. "There you go, ladies. I have a little boy around the same age, so I know what it's like when they're tired. Now, have a good day."

"Thank you." Feeling like a cross between a slimy snake and a low-life fraud, I returned her smile and followed Dana into the room.

The moment I closed the door behind me, Dana whipped Jake's battered dog out of her bag and, apologizing profusely, gave the toy back to him, wiped his eyes and planted a kiss on his damp cheek.

The howling stopped as if it had been knocked on the head with an iron bar.

"M-m-my doggo." Jake nestled the bedraggled toy to his chest and gave a toothy grin. I might have said it before, but boy, that kid was going to be a heart-breaker by the time he reached his teens.

"I know, I'm the Mother from Hell, and you're going to blame me for every bad choice you make in the years to come, aren't you?" Dana dug into her bag again, snaffled a Kit-Kat bar and peeled off the bright colored wrapping. "Here, darling," she handed her now-smiling son the chocolate bar. "Friends again?"

I guess they were as within seconds, most of the chocolate was smeared around Jake's mouth and his blah-colored dog had turned into a brown-spotted Dalmatian.

I gave the room a quick once-over. Typical $120 a night hotel-room. It had that vague smell of strangers having been here before you. Two-day-old socks, other people's sweat and maybe even a hint of old sex. Furniture consisted of a built-in wardrobe, chest of drawers, Queen-sized bed covered with a two-tone quilt, a lounge chair, a desk with a matching wooden chair and a 45-inch television fastened to the wall. A laptop and a large suitcase took up half the bed, the suitcase open and half-packed. Waiting for its owner to come up and finish the job.

"You take the chest-of drawers and his case. I'll check the wardrobe."

"Okay. Let's do it!" Dana dragged the suitcase across to her side of the bed and carefully, without displacing a thing, began exploring the contents. Watching her, I had to wonder if I really knew my friend. When *I* look through a suitcase, I either scrunch up everything, or upend the contents onto the bed and then have to repack. Not Dana. She lifted, checked and replaced every item so carefully, nothing looked disturbed. It was as though she'd been a spy in another life.

"Well, don't stand there gawking, see if his jacket's in the wardrobe. It's not here in the suitcase."

What was I doing, wasting time watching Dana? Our suspect could walk into the room at any minute. And if he found us here, in his room, looking for proof that he'd killed Petra, we'd be dry crumbly toast. Toast that he could crush in his hands and toss out the window for the birds.

Rousing myself, I slid the wardrobe door open and peered inside. The judge had been here for almost a week so there were several outfits, all on wire hangers. Three pairs of trousers, half a dozen shirts, a couple of suits – and there right at the end – a black jacket.

But was it the one we were looking for?

Jittering like a live wire in a thunderstorm, I lunged into the wardrobe, knocking a couple of shirts onto the floor in my haste, and dragged the jacket out. Almost afraid to look, I held the black jacket in the air, checked the buttons, and my heart immediately did a fast jog around the block.

Instead of six gold buttons, there were only five. One missing. Yanked off, leaving a jagged hole in the material.

I dug out my phone, clicked onto Album and scrolled down until the photo of the button from the alleyway popped up.

Yessss!

The gold button in the photo with the etchings around the outside matched the buttons on Hutchins' jacket.

"Oh, my God," whispered Dana, hot breath fanning my neck as she ogled over my shoulder. "It *is* him."

"Yes, Oliver T. Hutchins is Petra's killer."

"And *we* have the evidence."

At her words, a chill shot up my spine and anchored somewhere deep in my lungs causing my breathing to hitch and then momentarily stop. I gulped to set it going again. "Yeah, evidence that suddenly feels like a box full of venomous snakes." I could hear the shake in my voice but hey, it wasn't as bad as the shake in my hands as I placed Hutchins' jacket on the bed. "What do we do now?" I asked. "Ring the police and wait here for them to arrive?"

"Are you crazy?" Dana shot me one of famous 'looks' and grabbed the handle of Jake's stroller. "We get out of here. Fast." She leant over, whipped the jacket off the bed and shoved it into her bag with the baby wipes, bagged up wet nappies and all the other baby paraphernalia. "We'll take the jacket to the police station and tell them where we found it. Then *they* can come and arrest him."

"That's not going to work." I shook my head and frowned. "The police have to find Hutchins' jacket in his possession to charge him with Petra's murder." I hoped I was right. "So, I'll take a photo of his jacket with the button yanked off and then we'll put the evidence back in the wardrobe. Okay? And *then* hightail it to the nearest police station."

"You're right." She dragged the jacket out of her bag and held it in the air. "Quick, take a photo and then let's get out of here."

I aimed my phone in the direction of the jacket and snapped a couple of quick shots, but before Dana could return the evidence to the hotel wardrobe, she cocked one ear, listening.

A faint sound came from the corridor on the other side of the door.

I exchanged an *oh-hell-what-do-we-do-now* gawp with Dana and then, like in a Steven King horror movie, I watched the door handle edge millimeter by millimeter to the left. It was like staring into the hypnotic eyes of a giant crocodile and being unable to look away.

Someone was about to enter the room.

9

"Pssst! Abi? Dana? You in there?"

While my heart weighed up whether it was worthwhile starting to beat again, I let out a shaky breath and watched the door creak open, just enough to frame Molly's pale face.

Her eyes darted around the room as though she expected Hannibal Lecter to jump out at her, before they finally fastening on me. "It's only me."

"Geez, Molly, you almost made me wet my pants. What are you doing here? Where's Hutchins?"

Molly didn't move from the half-opened doorway. "That's what I came to tell you. I couldn't keep him talking any longer. He's on his way up. I beat him to the escalator and just managed to close the doors before he reached it." She took a quick glance over her shoulder. "But he'll definitely be on the next one."

"Holy crappola!" Dana hooked Hutchins' jacket onto the wardrobe rail and then, with Jake babbling away to Doggo, she maneuvered the pusher past Molly and was out the door before I could even get my immobilized feet unstuck from the floor.

Once moving, it took me no more than ten seconds to reach the lift – just as the smooth metal doors slid open.

And there he was – Oliver T. Hutchins.

The owner of the incriminating black jacket.

The monster who'd strangled Petra with an upmarket *Chanel* dog-leash.

Immediately, the hairs on the back of my neck woke up, took a peek at the scenery and began to shiver. Probably couldn't believe they were so up close and personal to a murderer. I blinked at him; throat too tight to speak. Or scream. Dressed in his gray trousers, blue and white striped shirt and well-polished, shiny black shoes, he looked so normal. So ordinary. How could that be? Why couldn't we see the beast that lay beneath that every-day mask?

The beast continued to stand there, arms folded, his yellow-green eyes narrowed dangerously, not attempting to alight from the lift. Was he going to whip out a gun from under his shirt and pop us off, one by one?

With a tiny whoosh, the hairs on the back of my neck dragged the covers over their head and started praying.

I was ready to join them.

After all, Hutchins was the sole occupant of the escalator. Our red-headed co-operative cleaner and her trolley were nowhere in sight. And the noise from the bar downstairs would drown out our screams.

We were on our own with a murderer.

"Wasn't I just talking to you downstairs?" Hutchins frown hit Molly between the eyes and then swiveled to rake across both Dana and me. "And don't I know you two?"

"Never seen you before," mumbled Dana, almost taking out his left foot in her haste to get Jake's pusher into the open lift. "Come on, ladies. If we don't hurry, we'll be late for that appointment I spoke about."

Not budging from the center of the escalator, Hutchins continued to frown at us. "I'm sure I've seen you ladies before."

I sidled past him, taking care that I didn't actually touch any of his murderer cooties, and plastered my hand over the down button, ready to push. "Sorry, Mister, but unless you want to go downstairs again, can you please get off? As my friend told you, we're running late."

"I know where I've seen you," he said, completely disregarding my words. "You were all showing your dogs under me last weekend at the Ladies Kennel Club show." His frown deepened as he stepped off the lift and turned to face us, suspicion written all over his face like it was printed in bright purple crayon. "So, what are you doing up here? What are you after?" He puffed out his chest, deepened his frown and leant forward. "Hey, have you been following me?"

I slammed my hand on the ground-floor button and the escalator door slid shut. But not quickly enough. Hutchins stuck his head and both arms through, yanking on the doors to open them again. I gasped and plastered my back up against the lift wall. But not Dana. With a yell that would have made Braveheart proud, she swung her king-sized bag like a baseball bat and caught him fair on the chin.

He let out a strangled *oomph* and the last we saw of him, just before the escalator doors slammed shut, he was staggering backwards holding his jaw with both hands.

"That should keep him occupied until the police arrive," said Dana hefting the bag back onto her shoulder.

I let out the breath I'd been holding and shook my head at her. "Ever thought of taking up women's baseball? You'd be the team's star batter and have agents clamoring to represent you."

Eyes twinkling, a broad grin spread across her face. "Felt pretty good actually. Reckon old Oliver T. might need to raid the freezer when he gets back to his room. See what he can find to ease the swelling in that chin."

Molly's high-pitched giggle sounded a little manic. "Or…if he's feeling anything like me, a glass of whisky and a good lie-down might be another option."

The moment the lift doors opened on the ground floor, we piled out and headed for the car park. Dana using Jake's stroller as a battering ram against anyone who got in her way, Molly and me following behind like a couple of red-faced bridesmaids, apologizing to those left with bruised body parts.

Half an hour later, after careering along Port Road at the razor-edge of the speed-limit, we pulled up outside the Port Adelaide police station. Although reporting our findings to the police was a priority, the three of us were also on a tight personal schedule. Molly needed to get back to Sebastian and Rebecca so she could fog up the page with the heat-level of their love-making. Dana was due to pick up her daughter, Kayla, from kindergarten at 3 o'clock. And I had to get my ass back to *The Pampered Pooch*. There was a delivery of new *Gucci* spring-fashion clothing for small dogs due to arrive, and my assistant couldn't serve customers, open the boxes and add the gorgeous creations to the clothing racks on her own. Plus, unpacking *Gucci's* new-season dog clothing was always a delight that left me smiling, and I didn't want Veronique cashing in on the pleasure.

After feeding two dollars into the parking meter, I led the way through the automatic doors and into the reception area, where a female police officer sat behind the front desk.

"Good afternoon, Ma'am," I said in my most polite, addressing-someone-in-authority voice. "We'd like to talk to Detective Inspector Lightfoot, please. It's urgent."

Due to my previous association with the detective, plus the incriminating photos saved to my cell phone, I'd been appointed official spokeswoman by our team.

"He's busy at the moment." The police-officer's eyes didn't move from her computer. "Please take a seat."

"I *did* say it was urgent."

She blew out a sigh but continued typing. "What is it you wish to speak to him about?"

"It's to do with the Petra Sullivan's murder."

She stopped typing long enough to lift one eyebrow at me. "What? You have new information to report?"

"Of course," put in Dana with a snort, conveniently forgetting I was the spokeswoman. She relieved Jake of a *Wanted* poster he'd commandeered from the front desk and substituted it with a small box of juice. "Otherwise we wouldn't be here, would we?"

I elbowed Dana in the ribs which set Jake giggling so much his juice spilled down the front of his Hairy McClary tee-shirt. "Can you please page Detective Lightfoot. Like, now. The murderer will be boarding a plane in a few hours, so time is of the essence."

A deep voice hailed from the other side of the room. A voice I recognized from the *Pussycat Parlor*. "What's this about the murderer boarding a plane?"

I spun around to find D.I. Lightfoot leaning against the jamb of an open doorway regarding me with a quizzical eyebrow.

"Ms. Truelove, isn't it?"

I nodded.

"Not a name I'd quickly forget." He folded his arms across his chest. "So, what have you been poking your nose into this time?"

Dana, one eye on the wall clock that proclaimed it was now 2.15 pm, butted in before I could think up an appropriate answer to his snide question. "Look, do you, or don't you want to know who murdered Petra Sullivan?" she said. "'Cos, if not, I really need to go pick up my daughter from kindergarten. I've been late twice this week and if I'm late again, it means my name goes up on their Naughty Mummy's Bulletin Board."

Lightfoot hauled his eyes across to Dana and I swear his lips twitched. "And you are?"

"Dana Fox, an associate of Ms. Truelove. And this is Molly Gibson," she pointed at Molly who looked like she was contemplating making a run for it before three sets of handcuffs made an appearance. "We're all members of the *Gumshoe Chicks*, and we have evidence that a show judge called Oliver T. Hutchins is guilty of murdering Petra Sullivan."

Before Molly could say, *I'm off home*, we found ourselves perched on hard wooden chairs in front of Lightfoot's desk. On the power side, the detective leaned back in his comfortable padded king-size chair, a small evidence bag with the gold button from the alleyway in one hand and my phone in the other.

"Well, well, well," he said at last, after studying first the gold button and then the photo of Hutchins' jacket. "This is very interesting." He cut his eyes to me. "And how did you say you came across this evidence?"

Damn. Should have seen that one coming. Skimming my rear to the edge of the chair in case a quick getaway was called for, I steamed right over his question by asking one of my own. "Do you agree it's the same gold button?" With any luck he'd be so happy with the results of this new evidence he wouldn't throw us in the slammer for break-and-enter.

"Hmm, of course we need this information verified by forensics, but yes, I'd say it is."

"So, if you're quick, you'll find the owner of that jacket camped in room 4 at the *Slug and Spinach*, 74 Kidman Road, Hindmarsh. The perp's name is Oliver T. Hutchins. He's a show judge who the deceased slept with in exchange for presenting her over-shot pug with the Best in Show trophy. And his plane to Sydney, Qantas, flight 21, is due to depart at 6 pm."

The DI frowned. "How did you acquire all this information?"

"Because that's what the *Gumshoe Chicks* do. We're unofficial private investigators." Dana, who was watching the hands of the wall clock as though they were fleas intent on infiltrating her hair-space, stood up and faced Jake's stroller in the direction of the door. "And now, I'm sorry, but I have to go. If my name goes up on the Naughty Mummy board again, that snooty-nosed Patricia Stamford of the *Canberra* Stamford's will have reason to emit that oh-so-smug, tinkly little laugh of hers, and *this* time, I might not be able to stop myself from shoving both her laugh and her tonsils right down her throat." She flicked her hair out of her eyes. "And then you'll have to lock me up in one of your cells. And you wouldn't want to do that, would you?"

The detective blinked, but evidently couldn't find any words to answer her question.

Molly was next to stand up, the legs of her chair making a scritching sound along the wooden floor. "Well, I'll leave it in your hands, Detective," she announced. "You're the policeman – I'm merely a romance writer. And if I don't hurry back to my two love-sick protagonists, they'll be too tired to co-operate in the next chapter. I left them trying out the first three positions of the Kama Sutra, but knowing Sebastian, they'll already be up to position 20." She scuttled past Jake's stroller and opened the door for Dana to exit before her.

DI Lightfoot's face reminded me of a surprised owl, his expression suggesting that I might actually be the least-crazy one of our threesome and he was finding that idea difficult to swallow. "Alright…Ms. Truelove, you may go too." He shook the confusion from his face, replacing it with a scowl and a strong jawline. "But don't think for a minute that we're done here. There are quite a few puzzling questions that need some answers."

I bet there were. And if it was up to me – they'd stay that way.

10

The subtle smell of vanilla and cosseted canine greeted me as I sprinted through the doors of *Pampered Pooch* ten minutes after the *Gucci* delivery was scheduled to arrive.

I sent a finger-wave to Veronique, who was busy re-pricing doggy denim jackets in the first aisleway. The jackets were included in a special two-day 25% off sale as they'd become a slow seller.

"You needn't have hurried, Abigail." She pointed to an unopened cardboard box on the floor near the counter. A stylish box with the distinguished *Gucci* logo. In her early fifties, Veronique was energetic, dressed to impress only herself, and always ready with either a joke or a supportive shoulder to lean on. She smiled and sent me a faint shoulder shrug. "Thought you needed something to cheer you up after last night's horror so I've kept my itchy fingers to myself."

"Thanks, Ronnie."

When Aunt Tilly died and I took over *Pampered Pooch*, Veronique had been like a fairy godmother to me. Without her friendship, expertise and knowledge of accounts and what was likely to sell and what wasn't, the boutique would have gone bankrupt within the first months. Now, after working together for two years, we'd become even closer.

And I adored everything about *Pampered Pooch*.

A policy I'd set up not long after taking over was to encourage customers to bring their pampered pooches to the boutique. After all, if a dog owner intended to buy a new rug, a special toy or a trendy doggy-ballet dress for that upcoming party, why not ensure the recipient had a say in the selection. Only one rule – no aggression tolerated. Any bad-mannered canine was hit with a life-time ban. No second chances. No get-out-of-jail-free card. However, we'd only ever had trouble with one dog, a rat-faced Chihuahua named Sugarlumps, who was a re-incarnated Rottweiler-guard-dog. However, due to his diminutive size he'd been spared the ban but was only allowed in the shop on the condition he stayed inside his owner's bag at all times.

In front of a sign proclaiming, *Pampered Pooch Toys – Let the fun begin,* I spotted an animated French Bulldog racing up and down, snorting and panting and grinning, all at the same time. I smiled. It was Louis, one of my favorite doggy customers. By the length of his tongue, I guessed he was excited at being allowed to choose his own toy.

Louis's owner, Sally Tregenza, a newbie to the dog show world, stood patiently waiting for him to make up his mind. Her arms were already piled high with other doggy merchandise. "You can only pick one today, Louis. You already have a room full of toys at home."

The little dog had narrowed his choice down to a multi-colored caterpillar three times his size and a fluffy chicken that squawked like he'd spotted a fox near the henhouse, every time his tummy was squeezed.

In the finish it was a no-brainer. Frenchy chose the squawker, then, chicken in his mouth, he trotted up to me and grinned around the yellow fluff.

"Hi, Louis. Good choice." I grinned down at the little brindle dog with the squashed in nose. His oversized ears stood to attention and his little black eyes twinkled up at me. French bulldogs were so cute and Louis was the cutest of them all. "Now," I said, pretending to treat him like a regular customer. "Will that be cash or credit card today, sir?"

"Make it credit card." Sally answered for him as she trotted along behind her pride and joy. "And if I don't start leaving Louis home when

I come here, my credit will end up in the red. He already has a room full of toys to play with but every time he enters your shop, he sneaks a new one from your display." She leant down and tickled the little dog under his chin. "But who can refuse that adorable face?"

"Not you, evidently." I chuckled as I rang up one red velvet collar, a bag of caviar treats, a Vera Wang coffee mug with the image of a French Bulldog on the front, plus the chicken that Louis had decided was going to take roost in his toy room.

"Actually, I didn't expect to see you in here today." Sally's face softened as she glanced up from swiping her card through the machine. "I heard on the news that you found Petra Sullivan's body. Must have been awful for you."

"Awful doesn't begin to describe it."

I didn't want to talk about the 'body'. It was still far too raw in my mind. The dead eyes, the broken teeth, a dog-leash exactly like those we sold in our shop, knotted around her neck. We'd had a run of people at the boutique earlier in the day, not looking to buy, but to interrogate and gossip and I wasn't ready to elaborate. Then, or now.

Sally leant closer so she could whisper in my ear. "Don't tell anyone, but I was at *The Pussycat Parlor* Saturday night too. Met up with six old school friends. See, we get together three or four times a year and this time it was Mad Marcia's turn to choose the location. Naturally, she didn't opt for a nice dinner at a respectable restaurant, or a night out at the theatre. Oh, no, Marcia opted for a nightclub. And not just any old nightclub. She chose *The Pussycat Parlor*. A club that's notorious for its glamorous strippers and pole-dancers and where it seems like anything goes." She sighed. "My boyfriend, Sean, he wasn't happy about it, was he? Got all huffy about me going to a club. But hey, the damp mop never takes me anywhere exciting and we need lives away from each other as well. Don't we?"

I nodded. In my case, as far away as possible.

"Thing is, we left just after midnight, you know, like Cinderella, so missed all the excitement." She dipped her head as if to confide further.

"You are *so* lucky to have a boyfriend who takes you to these places. Sean's such a stick-in-the-mud. Sometimes I think he needs a firecracker up his backside."

"Luke's the same. His idea of a good night out is watching the Crows beat the Port in a footy game."

Sally blinked. "But I saw Luke at the club. Wasn't he there with you?"

"Um…yes. Of course."

So, Luke *was* at the *Pussycat Parlor*. Did he have anything to do with Petra's murder? Did she reject him, so he strangled her? I sighed. No, of course not. Luke wasn't capable of murder. Geez, I'd lived with the guy, so I'd know if he was a potential Jack the Ripper, wouldn't I? I had to stop thinking of everyone I knew as a prospective murderer. It was Oliver T. who offed Petra, and we'd just given the police evidence to prove it. Luke must have gone straight to the club to tell Petra he was moving in with her when he left my house.

As I bagged up Sally's purchases, I deliberately changed the subject. I'd had my fill of murder-talk for the day. "By the way, Sally, congratulations on Louis winning Best of Breed and gaining the final points for his championship title at the show last weekend." I smiled down at the comical little dog whose mouth was overflowing with fluffy yellow chicken. "So, *Australian Champion Somerset Louis the Lip*. Sounds good, doesn't it? Have you entered him again for next Saturday's show?"

"No. He's a funny little guy. The breeder who I bought him from said he gets bored and doesn't perform well if he's shown too often."

"You're doing the right thing then, Sally. There are quite a few competitors out there who run their dogs around the ring week in, week out, but their beautifully groomed aristocrats look more like they're heading for a stuffy museum than having a fun day out at a dog show.

As I turned to wave goodbye to Sally and her newly titled champion, I eyed the pink and white *Gucci* box still waiting for me to unpack its special delights. All those little dresses and suits and party clothes and the alternative colorful bandanas for those not so much into dressing up.

Couldn't wait.

As usual, before I slid the point of my scissors through the seal, I singled out a pair of fine plastic gloves from the drawer and tugged them on. Hey, some of these creations, being exclusive, would set a buyer back up to $2000, so it was important to show respect for the product.

"How did your meeting go with the girls?" Veronique, who'd finished pricing the sale items, had begun bagging liver treats nearby. "Any clues?"

I lifted an eyebrow and, bursting to spit out our latest news, launched a Cheshire Cat grin in her direction. "*Any clues*?" I repeated her words in a mock-patronizing voice. "Hey, we, the *Gumshoe Chicks*, solved the mystery, single-handed."

"Nooo!"

"Yeees! It was the show-judge, the guy Petra slept with to win Best in Show."

"Oliver Hutchins?" Veronique, a frown etched across her forehead, rubbed a finger along the side of her nose. "But why would *he* strangle her? That's not usually a follow-up to fun in the bedroom."

My euphoria did a sudden nose-dive. I scowled at her. Veronique was sucking the satisfaction out of my announcement. "Okay...we don't know his motive as yet, but we *did* find Oliver's jacket in the hotel room where he's staying, minus a button. And guess what? The buttons on his jacket match the button found in the alleyway beside Petra's body."

"Well done."

I picked up my cell phone, checked the time and grinned at her. "And round about now, the police should be storming the *Slug and Spinach,* charging Oliver with murder and clamping him in irons." I carefully extracted a gorgeous beach outfit, complete with sun hat, suitable for a toy-sized pampered pooch and slipped it onto a silk-covered hanger, before turning back to my all-ears assistant. "And do you know the best part? Now that Petra's murderer is behind bars, that snippy detective with the icy eyes reinforced with steel, won't have any reason to shoot me full of questions anymore."

"Don't put the cart before the horse, Abi. You're not out of the snippy detective's radar, just yet. As well as the evidence you found, unless the plaintiff confesses, the police will need to examine alibi, opportunity and motive."

"Well, Oliver definitely had opportunity. He was in the club that night, I saw him. And the angry glare he was firing at Petra should have annihilated her on the spot." To me, the case was cut and dried. Oliver T. was guilty. End of story. Veronique was just being finicky. "And motive could have been anything, from rejection to blackmail. Petra wasn't exactly Miss Sunshine and Flowers when it came to hurting people's feelings."

"All I'm saying, is, don't put your investigator's hat away just yet." And then she put her arms around me and gave me a quick cuddle and I realized, as usual, Veronique was only looking out for me.

The rest of the afternoon passed in a busy blur. As well as unpacking, admiring, and arranging the new *Gucci* fashionwear, we were invaded by a boisterous bus-load of retirees from a nearby nursing home, all cashed up and intent on spending big dollars on their newly acquired rescue dog, Sinatra, as they called him. A canine jigsaw-puzzle, the dog had long droopy ears like a beagle, a body built like a bulldog and a short curly tail leading me to wonder if maybe a pig got lose in the kennel-house during the mating.

So, three hours later, as I cruised into my driveway and parked the van in front of the carport, I was ready to grab a coffee and a donut, put my feet up on the pouffe and spend an hour on my phone, checking messages and maybe uploading a few photos of Sinatra the Mutt on *Pampered Pooch's* Facebook page.

As I dragged myself toward the front door, a familiar black, white and teal football jumper attached to a well-known body stepped out from behind the bushes.

"Luke?"

What the heck was Luke doing here?

"Hi babe," he said, his smile dialed up to 100 watts as he hefted an arm around my shoulders. "I've been thinking. Let's put this Petra business behind us, shall we? She was bad news and sucked me in." When I tried to dislocate his shoulder while hurling his arm as far away from me as I could, he put on an affronted woe-is-me face. "Come on, Abi, don't be like that. I'm big enough to admit I was in the wrong, but it wasn't all my fault. You aren't always easy to live with, you know."

I sent him a chilled-to-the-bone glare. "If I was a schoolteacher grading this apology, Luke, I'd need another letter below Z."

"Just return my key, okay, and I'll move my stuff back in. It probably would have been a disaster living with Petra anyway, and now she's dead, the landlord won't let me stay there."

"In that case, it looks like you'll have to shift back in with your parents, because I'd rather swallow the damn key than give it back to you." Fingers tightly clutched around my front door key, I pressed it deeper into my pocket. "You said you loved Petra, so where's the show of grief? The hand-wringing? The tears? Why aren't you upset about your girlfriend's death?"

"Look, about Petra being my girlfriend. You shouldn't have told the police about me and Petra." He shook his head at me. "I had a detective drop into my work-place this morning. Very embarrassing. He was questioning me on my whereabouts last night."

"And?"

"I told him I was nowhere near the Pussycat Parlor. I was home with you."

"You told the police you were home with me? Are you crazy? For a start, I wasn't home at 1 am – I was in an alleyway at the back of the nightclub, staring down at a pair of dead eyes and a face that looked like it had gone ten rounds with Mohamad Ali. And you weren't home – you were seen inside the club by one of my customers."

"You bitch. After all I've done for you." Luke's face twisted and for a moment I thought he was going to hit me. Instead, he grabbed my wrist, his fingers digging into the skin.

"Let me go, Luke. I have no more to say to you. It's over. We're finished."

"But, Abi I–"

A sleek silver Lexus that made my much-loved, but three-year-old van look at least in need of a paint job, glided quietly to a halt in my driveway. No one I knew. I squinted to see who was behind the wheel, but the windows were tinted, and I couldn't see a thing. My heart did a panicked flip-flop as I debated on who could be calling on me at six o'clock in the evening, in a luxury five-figure vehicle.

Was my visitor a crime-boss from the Mafia, mistaking me for a stoolie? Or a sour-faced accountant from the Taxation Department demanding he check my books?

I punched Luke's arm to loosen his grip and swiveled around for a better view of the driver as he stepped from the car and strode across my little patch of lawn towards us. And immediately decided the face attached to the powerfully built guy in an expensive silver-blue suit, was anything but sour.

God-like maybe, film-star-gorgeous perhaps, but definitely not sour.

My insides clenched, and I swear I was about to have one of those hot flushes my mother is always complaining about as I ogled the way the guy's muscles rippled under that beautifully tailored suit.

Beside me, Luke let go of my wrist and took a step away, eyes riveted on the newcomer, who'd muscled right into his space.

"I heard the lady ask you to leave," he said in a voice that dripped with chocolate. Or maybe steel, whichever side of the fence you were on.

"What's it to you, buddy?"

"I heard there was a disturbance at this address." The God in a Suit whipped a police identity warrant from an inner pocket, flashed it past Luke's eyes so quickly it barely disturbed the air and with an almost magical hey-presto, returned the card from whence it came.

I blinked, did a double take, as recognition slammed into me and left me spluttering. Had to wipe my hand across my mouth to cover the grin.

"Right, I'll say this only one more time, sir." The policeman's head was high, his jaw granite. Such a good actor. "I want you to leave. Now."

Luke 's lip trembled like a little boy with no presents at Christmas. "But I live here," he wailed.

Suit-guy turned to me with raised eyebrows and an almost undetectable smirk itching away at the corners of his lips. "Is that right, madam?"

"No, sir." This was turning into one of those farcical Noel Coward plays I'd studied at school. "This man doesn't live here anymore."

"Hey, don't listen to her. I'm her boyfriend, Luke Brody. We're just having a little misunderstanding. That's all."

"Little misunderstanding?" I rounded on him, both fists in the Queensbury Rules position. If the nice policeman hadn't been watching so intently, I might have followed through with a right uppercut. "Luke, you were bonking Petra, the pole-dancing stripper, for two months before I found out. If that's a little misunderstanding, I'm Princess Leia from *Star Wars*."

"I want my key back."

Like magic, a pair of handcuffs appeared under Luke's nose. "Sir, the only thing you'll be receiving is a restraining Order to stay away from your ex. Definitely no key. And, if you're still here by the time I count to five, you'll be accompanying me to the station to see a man about renting a cell for the night. A cell already occupied by a rather dirty, smelly drunk. One…two…three…"

Luke's shoulders drooped and he let out a full-bodied sigh like his world had just come tumbling down around him. I even felt a tiny twinge of sympathy. But only a twinge – not a genuine actual bona fide authentic emotion.

"Okay, okay, I'm going." Waving a virtual white flag, he turned to me. "I'm sorry, Abi, I truly am. I admit Petra was an addiction I couldn't resist. Like hard drugs." He dug his hands in his pocket and kicked at a stone. "Not to talk ill of the dead, but at least she can't hurt anyone now."

He let out another dramatic sigh and when I didn't respond, turned away and trudged toward his car which was parked on the street a couple of houses away.

I smiled up at Nathan Forrester, the private investigator who'd asked me to ring him if I broke up with Luke. The man who charged $300 an hour to investigate. "Since when do private investigators carry fake police warrants and handcuffs?"

"Since they discovered how well they work in the PI business." He cut me a wink as we continued to watch Luke walk away. "Now, as it seems your boyfriend is not your boyfriend any more, before I leave, how about instead of ringing, I ask you out for dinner, face-to-face?"

"Or," I said, peering up at him through my not-so-long luscious lashes. "We could take this discussion inside my house and decide the day, the time, and the restaurant, while partaking of a glass of wine."

Ha. Couldn't have expressed it better if the wording had been scripted for a movie.

While digging the front door key from the depths of my coat pocket, I checked out my ex's slumped shoulders as he opened his car door. After today's scenario, it was like I'd never really known him. Admittedly he hated losing, whether it was in football or life, but he'd never shown aggression to me before. And why did he lie to the police about where he was at the time Petra was murdered? Why did he say he was home with me when he was at the club?

An uneasy feeling, like a cold-blooded, wart-ridden cane-toad brushed up against my skin. I shuddered.

If I didn't know for a fact that we'd already unearthed our murderer, I'd be adding a big red asterisk right beside Luke Brody's name on my suspect list.

11

Chloe and Mimi were going crazy on the other side of the front door, yapping and frantically scratching at the paint. Chloe because raised voices stressed her out. Mimi, because she was Mimi. I slid the key into the keyhole, and the moment the door opened and I floated inside, followed by Mr. Private Investigator, the frenzied barking devolved into little whimpers, squeals and furry-dervish love squeaks.

But the love wasn't aimed at yours truly.

It was all for Nathan Forrester.

"You some kind of dog whisperer?" I asked as I observed Mimi, the unpredictable orange-colored fluff ball, attempt to not *bite* Nathan's leg, but use it as a ladder to climb up into his arms. "I can't believe that dog isn't chomping bits off your ankle and spitting them into her feed bowl."

Even Chloe, who normally kept tripping me over in her delight at having me home after a day at work, allotted me one sloppy hello-smooch and then, ears flapping, eyes starry with excitement, nudged Mimi out the way so she had more room to climb up Nathan's other leg.

Of course, neither dog could reach much further than a few inches above his knee before slipping off again. But the objective was clear to see.

They wanted up. In his arms. For cuddles.

I hadn't expected Nathan Forrester to be an animal magnet. My only association with him prior to tonight, was as a prospective client. And while in his office, behind that large chrome desk, the hot P.I. had struck me as a guy who would always maintain his coolness and elegance, in any situation. But looking at him now, his grin was real, his delight at the two overexcited dogs was real. And I could feel my growing attraction to the guy was one-hundred-percent real.

I eyed off the silver-blue suit that fit him like a team of tailors had spent weeks perfecting the way it hung, and ran a hand through my hair. Surprise didn't cut it. I wouldn't have blamed him if he'd used a kitchen chair to keep the attackers at bay. Hey, if *my* outfit cost more than I earned in a month, I'd be keeping away from dog nails and hair like the plague. Not Nathan. First, he lifted up stumpy-legged Chloe who wriggled and squirmed her deep chested body in delight as he kissed her on the nose, before placing her carefully back down again. Then he picked up Mimi and repeated the action. How come Mimi didn't bite off his nose and use it to poke out his eye? I was a dog lover and the little hell-fire treated me like a human dart board – and that was when she was being sociable at meal times.

"We always had dogs in the house when I was growing up," he said smiling down at Chloe, who'd raced off to her toy box and returned with her favorite green and yellow wooly ball for Nathan to throw. "I've missed having them around since I got a life of my own."

Here was a chance to learn more about that 'life of his own'. I ditched my handbag and laptop on the coffee table and moved across to the drinks' cabinet. "Why couldn't you have dogs when you moved into your own home?"

"My wife loathed anything with hair. Including me, as it turned out."

"Oh, I'm sorry."

So much for learning more about that 'life of his own'.

He scooped up Chloe's wooly ball and bowled it along the floor for both dogs to chase. "Nothing to be sorry about. The marriage only lasted six months and we've been divorced for several years now."

"So, why no dogs now you live on your own?"

His mouth turned up into a crooked half-smile. "I don't know, guess I just never got around to it."

"Seems a shame."

"Not all doom and gloom though. I still get my doggy buzz whenever

I visit my parents."

I cut him a smile. "So, after all these years, your parents still have dogs in the house?"

"You'd love my parents, Abi. You have so much in common with them." He bent to retrieve the ball from Mimi's mouth – how he still managed to retain all his fingers after that little act of bravery I don't know – and tossed it along the floor again. "My mother recently became a soft-touch for retired racing greyhounds. Over the last year, she and Dad have adopted four – couldn't stop at one, of course – and every one of them go bananas when they hear my car pull up outside the house. As soon as Mum opens the front door, there's a mad race to the car to be first in line for cuddles and ear rubs. Greyhounds are great dogs. And they make the best pets."

"I know. Dana has a pet greyhound called Penelope. She was bred for showing, so she's a slightly different shape to the racing greyhound, but has the same beautiful temperament." I shook my head as an image of Jake chewing on the end of poor Penelope's tail popped into my head. "And with two small kids in the house, she'd need to be."

Nathan's slow grin lit up those expressive sea-green eyes that seemed to be following my every movement. "Yes, I've met the extremely tolerant Penelope and would be the first to advocate sainthood for that dog."

I wandered over to the drink's cabinet and after selecting two bottles of wine, held them up for Nathan to inspect. "Red or white? I'm afraid they're only bottle shop quality, but they do the trick."

"Whatever you're having is fine with me."

I watched him settle into the nearest lounge chair, lean back, and cross his legs at the ankles. Legs that I could imagine wrapped around me. Naked. In bed. I licked my dry lips. Slapped the images away as far-too-soon. "I'm confused," I said, swallowing the heat in my throat. "How did you know to pull up in my driveway at exactly the same time Luke was proving difficult? Were the neighbors really complaining?"

His deep chocolatey laugh set my heart fluttering, brought the far-too-soon images tumbling back. "Complete coincidence," he assured me. "I bumped into Peter, Dana's husband, and he told me you'd broken up with Luke."

"And they say women gossip."

"Well, I thought about it for a while, maybe three minutes, and then decided not to wait for you to ring me. Too hit and miss. Instead, I opted to drop around to your house and ask you out for dinner myself."

I couldn't stop the gooey smile from taking control of my lips.

"And then, when I pulled up in your driveway and saw you having problems with your ex., I was left with no alternative but to don my PI hat and move him on, pronto." He raised one teasing eyebrow. "Which gave you *another* reason to say yes to a dinner date with me."

I laughed. "Did you see Luke's face when you dragged out those handcuffs?" *Almost like he had something to hide. But what?* "Geez, what if he'd had a coronary and I had to ring the ambulance. How would you have explained the fake police ID then?"

"Poor guy must have imagined it. All I had in my possession was my Private Investigator ID." He fastened two mock-serious eyes on me. "Now, think carefully, Ms. Truelove. Did I mention the word 'police' when I pulled my card out?"

The rich chocolatey voice I'd loved from the moment I heard Nathan on the phone was even more seductive when it became playful.

By now, Chloe and Mimi were tugging on the ends of his trousers, vying for his attention. I reached for the treat jar. "Sorry about that, Nathan. I'll put these little guys outside. Chloe is normally very well-mannered in company, but the fluffy demon-from-hell is a bad influence. Mimi isn't mine. I'm only babysitting her until her owner is released from jail."

"Sounds interesting." He cocked his head to the side in a tell-me-more gesture before settling more comfortably in the lounge chair.

"Interesting doesn't begin to describe it!"

After enticing Chloe and Mimi out the back door with a handful of treats, I poured two glasses of white wine, flopped into my favorite chair, and told Nathan the story of my introduction to Mimi's owner, *Pussy Willow*, via a murdered body in the laneway at the back of her workplace.

His frown was full of concern. "That must have been a nightmare for you."

"You're not wrong there. Anyway, it was Sharon who noticed the clue. A gold button lying beside the body. I was too distraught to see anything except Petra's dead staring eyes."

I went on to tell him how the police took the stripper off to jail for tampering with evidence at the crime scene, how Dana, Molly, and I followed up on the clue and how we'd traced the incriminating button back to Oliver T. Hutchins, the show judge who'd awarded Petra's dog Best in Show after sleeping with her. "And, thanks to us, right now, Petra's murderer should be getting locked in a cell at the police station."

Nathan was a good listener, commenting only when he didn't fully understand the picture. However, it was his sea-green eyes that kept leading me astray. They were so expressive, so inviting, that a number of times I hesitated, imagined myself sitting on his lap and kissing him senseless. Very distracting.

Finally, Mr. Distraction himself, a slight twist to the corners of his lips as though he could read my X-rated thoughts, broke in. "And did you see the accused at the nightclub on the night of Petra's murder?"

I nodded. "Oliver's eyes were glued to Petra. And it wasn't her pole dancing expertise that was fascinating him. He seemed furious, absolutely livid with her about something. And whatever that something was, it's most likely his motive for killing her."

My phone chirped and a text came through.

It was from Dana.

Urgent. Go check your emails and then ring me back.

I frowned. Re-read the text. "It's from Dana," I told Nathan, and passed my phone across to him. "Look, I'm sorry, but I need to turn on my laptop. I keep my emails on there so they're safe, you know, for work and taxation purposes. God knows what's got Dana in such a flap."

He read the text and after placing my cell on the coffee table between us, went to stand up. "Look, I'll get going. What if I ring you later and we make a time to pick you up for dinner tomorrow night?"

"No, please, stay. Just until I find out what's going on with Dana. My friend is usually so down to earth and unshakeable. The word 'urgent' isn't normally part of her vocabulary."

He nodded and dropped back into the chair. "You're right. I thought it might have been a girly thing, but as you say, that's not like Dana. She sounds really upset."

It took less than a minute to snaffle my laptop from the coffee table, open it and bring up my emails.

I quickly scrolled through my incoming mail, stopping at an email that made me almost choke on my spit. The email had been sent a little over three hours ago and it was from a known name in my address book – Oliver T. Hutchins.

TO MY FRIENDS, ENEMIES AND COLLEAGUES:

Today is my last day on earth. Why? Because I am a murderer and can't live a lie any longer. I killed Petra Sullivan and therefore I must end my life too.

I put Petra's pug up for Best in Show, even though it has the worst underbite I have ever seen. But I was obsessed with Petra and promised her the trophy in exchange for a night of passion. For me it was love but for Petra it was a means to an end. She videoed us having sex and then blackmailed me, threatening to upload the video online. I couldn't let her do that. She had to die.

After much soul-searching, I've decided I can't live my life jumping at shadows any longer and I am too much of a gentleman to survive in jail. Plus, orange doesn't suit me.

Goodbye.

Oliver T. Hutchins.

"Oh, my God." Mouth opening and shutting like a beached tuna, I blinked across the coffee table at Nathan. "Oliver T. Hutchins, the show-judge, has committed suicide."

12

Two hours later, I sat, stretched out in my favorite chair, the big flowery monstrosity that turned into a day bed if I pressed a button on the side. It had been my Aunt Tilly's favorite when she was alive, and when I inherited her house, it became mine.

"Holy freakin' Zeus!" Dana, legs tucked under her on the chair beside me, downed her third glass of wine and looked to the heavens – or in this case the sky-blue ceiling of my loungeroom – then rolled her eyes at Molly sprawled on the couch, opposite. "The man is a murderer." She said each word slowly, distinctly, like she was talking to Kayla, her three-year-old daughter. "He's one of the bad guys. Why are you defending him, Molly?"

"Because *we* killed him." Molly returned Dana's eye-roll with an extra rotation before licking the lip of her empty wineglass. A party trick she performed whenever she drank wine. "*We* forced that man to take his own life."

Dana's mouth went into fly-catching mode. "You're joking! How?"

"Think about it, Dana. When the elevator doors opened and Oliver saw us standing there, looking guilty, he must have guessed what we'd been up to. That we'd been rummaging around in his room and spotted his jacket, minus the incriminating button."

"So?"

"*So*, he knew we were on our way to the police station. You know, to dob him in."

"And your point is?"

"We left that poor man in an emotional state, contemplating jail, and knowing he wouldn't survive in there with all those nasty criminal types." Molly wrapped her arms around her upper-body and gave a dramatic shiver. "So, the moment the elevator goes down, he returns to his room, sees we've been in there, sends off a confession to everyone in his contact list, then puts a gun to his head and pulls the trigger." She lifted one shoulder in a questioning shrug. "How can we live with that?"

"Easily." Dana leant forward in her chair, all the better to get into Molly's personal space. "Killing himself was *his* decision, not ours – like the decision he made in the back alley of the *Pussycat Parlor* when he enticed Petra away from the safety of the club, coiled a dog leash around her neck and then jerked it so tight she gave up breathing. Like forever."

"But now there's *two* people dead," wailed Molly, bestowing one last lick to the top of her empty glass before almost missing the table as she set it down. Molly's drinking was as unsophisticated as her invisible sex life. One glass of wine, she turned into a bubbly teenager. Two glasses of wine she became overemotional. And, if she bottomed out and downed a third, she'd be sleeping on my couch, her snoring comparable to heavy-duty machinery, until the following morning.

I sat back and allowed the conversation to pass over me without contributing an opinion. Okay, I didn't feel any guilt about Oliver's death, but it had knocked me for a loop when I'd first read that email. Sent me mentally sprawling like the skittles in a bowling alley. After all, it's not every day you open your inbox to find one of your contacts has sent you their last email, ever. A contact who was dead before the email even landed in your computer.

If I'd been alone, I'd have freaked out, big time. But with Nathan's strong arms wrapped around me in a warm hug, his rich chocolatey voice in my ear, calming me down, I'd eventually stopped shaking long enough to ring Dana and Molly and arrange a meeting. Nathan stayed with me right up until Molly arrived in her little toy car demanding to know why she'd been pulled away from her Kama-Sutra-gorged lovers. Again. While Dana had heard the news on the television, hence her text to me, Molly had been unaware of Oliver's suicide.

Then, after Nathan left, first dropping a light kiss on my lips that made me wish he'd forget our relationship was so new it was barely out of its wrapper and let the kiss deepen, flood me with his heat, I filled Molly in on the newest turn of events. She didn't take it well. Luckily, Dana, armed with two bottles of Turkey Flat, her favorite wine, had trooped in ten minutes later, and helped calm Molly down. As neither child was tagging along behind her, Peter must have been allocated bath, bed and story-reading duties for the night.

That was two hours and three glasses of wine ago.

Now, with Chloe curled up on my lap, sound asleep after her hectic Mimi-filled day, my eyes kept returning to the chilling message staring back at me from the screen of my open laptop.

For the umpteenth time, I studied the words in Oliver's email. There was something bugging me about it. Something that didn't quite ring true. "Petra's pug," I said, screwing up my eyes in concentration, "hasn't she got an *over*bite?"

Dana nodded. "That dog's overbite is so bad Petra had to puree her food so she could eat."

"But Oliver's saying she's got an *under*bite."

"Where?" Dana screwed the laptop around so she could read the email again.

"See." I pointed to the screen and then read the words aloud. *I put Petra's pug up for Best in Show, even though it has the worst underbite I have ever seen.* Why would he say that? Oliver's a professional judge. He's judged at international dog shows in both America and Europe. Even if he only did a perfunctory examination of the dog before winking at Petra and then declaring her pug Best in Show, he'd notice the dog had an *over*bite."

"Hmm. I see your point."

"However," put in Molly, quick to air her views. "You're both forgetting one thing. It's a suicide note. He'd be shaking, thinking more of the gun lying in wait for him than the shape of Petra's pug's mouth. *Under* bite. *Over* bite. Who cares? It was more than likely just spellcheck being over-enthusiastic, as usual."

Molly was probably right. If Oliver intended to kill himself after crafting the email, his brain would have already been deep fried and over-cooked. God knows how he managed to think at all.

I read the message again. And chewed on a hangnail. Nah.…I still wasn't completely convinced. And there it was. Another discrepancy. More wording that wasn't Oliver's. "What about this bit?" I pointed again and read aloud. "*…and I am too much of a gentleman to survive in jail. Plus, orange doesn't suit me.*" Does that sound like stuffy old Oliver to you?" I shook my head and answered my own question. "No, it doesn't. If he ever cracked a joke, his pants would fall down. And as for him being flippant a couple of minutes before blowing his brains out…I don't think so."

Dana re-filled her glass and asked with a lift of her chin if I wanted mine topped up too. I shook my head. Completely ignoring Molly's empty glass as an accident waiting to happen, she returned the wine bottle to the table. "So, what are you trying to tell us, Abi? That Oliver was out of his mind when he tapped out his last words?"

"I'm saying…the correspondence I received from Oliver while organizing his show-schedule…well…it was nothing like this. His emails were so full of stuffy jargon and long-winded waffle, I sometimes struggled to comprehend what the heck the guy was getting at." I stopped, rearranged my thoughts, before plunging on. "What I'm saying, I suppose, is that the words in that email are definitely not Oliver's."

"Whaaat?" Molly's voice choked as though she'd swallowed several passing flies and they were currently picnicking in her windpipe. "Do you mean someone else wrote that suicide note?"

"I guess I am."

"But-but that would mean…"

I nodded, my heartbeat slowing right down like it was wading through thick mud in Louboutin high heels. "Oliver didn't kill Petra and he didn't kill himself."

Molly's face went a shade of white I didn't think existed. "And we helped the real murderer set Oliver up?"

I nodded. The lump in my throat blocking any other answer.

"Not necessarily!" said Dana, with her usual *Gumshoe Chick* logic. "Oliver could have killed Petra and then someone else killed him to avenge her murder."

"Like one of her gazillion sexual conquests?"

"Yeah, and he made it look like a suicide so that he would never be found out."

"Hmm…unlikely, though. I'd reckon ninety-nine percent of her conquests would be so relieved to find themselves off the hook, they'd be applauding Oliver, not killing him. Petra had a cute way of emasculating men once she finished using them. She'd spit them out, compare their love-God to a soft and squishy licorice stick, and then blackmail them into adding monthly payments to her bank account in return for not informing their wives or girlfriends. No, I'm more inclined to believe one person is responsible for both murders."

"Holy freakin' Zeus!" Dana's brow creased as though she'd been hit with a two by four. "I've just had a thought. What if Oliver's murderer was already at the *Slug and Spinach* when we arrived? What if he or she was watching us, laughing at how easily we'd fallen into their trap? How we'd been led to the 'planted' clue, the gold button, put two and two together and came up with the wrong answer?"

I shivered like I'd been soaking in an ice bath. "And as soon as we left, he or she rode up in the elevator, broke into Oliver's room and killed him."

Molly's wail could have been heard five blocks away as she snatched the wine bottle off the coffee table and upended the contents straight down her throat.

I let out an almighty sigh. All that wine would see Molly sleeping on my couch tonight, but me, I didn't think I'd ever sleep again.

Why?

Because, either way, there was a killer on the loose – one who might now decide to come after us.

*****

Getting ready for work the next morning was proving more difficult than catching a dragon with a butterfly net.

As well as my normal early morning activities, there was both Molly and Mimi to contend with. Molly, propped up on my couch, her face the color of two-minute noodles, hands clasping her head – probably to prevent it from falling off – was demanding a never-ending supply of caffeine. While Mimi, the demented orange fluff-ball, wearing the same Winnie the Pooh PJ's she'd arrived in, was in a right-royal 'snit'.

How did Dana, with two kids clogging up her daily schedule, manage to always appear cool and competent, as though she'd stepped out of a fashion magazine? Even when there was a blob of some unknown grey/green/purple substance decorating the front of her shirt?

"No, Mimi!" I yelped, dodging another snarling attack that included teeth sharpened to vampire points heading in the direction of my ankles. "You can't have another helping of Doggy Doo Dry. You've already eaten breakfast."

Mimi's serial-killer eyes closed into narrow slits as she glared at me, her top lip curled, displaying every battle-ready tooth in her head. Knowing she was the winner before the war even began, she let out a volley of high-pitched, glass-cracking yaps.

"Oooh, Abi, please, please, *please*, make that dog stop," moaned the ghost-like figure from the couch. "One more bark and my head's going to explode all over your lounge-room walls."

And I didn't want that...

I let out a sigh of resignation. Hoisted the white flag. Dragged the box of Doggy Doo's down from the top shelf and filled Mimi's food bowl. Again. What else could I do? I didn't have the contact number for the priest at the local church and even if I did, I had a feeling he wouldn't be willing to perform an early-morning exorcism in order to purge an exploding head due to a hangover.

Total wins since yesterday: Mimi eleven – Abi none.

After returning the now half-empty Doggy Doo packet to the top shelf of my kitchen cupboard, I rummaged around in my handbag. Cell phone – check. Car keys – check. Printed copy of Oliver's fake email with suspect wording underlined in red – check. Then I ferried one last cup of coffee and a dry cracker biscuit to Molly and unhooked two dog leads from behind the kitchen door.

Not only was I running late for work, I also had to visit the police station beforehand. Lucky me. I'd been elected by the *Gumshoe Chicks* to front up to DI Lightfoot and point out the inconsistencies in Oliver's email. Convince him that the dead man didn't write that suicide note.

As I said: *Lucky me...*

The vote hadn't even been conducted fairly, you know, by putting three names in a hat and pulling one name out. No – it was me or no one. When Molly finished off the last bottle of Turkey Flat wine, we knew she'd be in no condition to do anything but vomit, moan and drink coffee this morning, while Dana's mobile dog wash, *Hydro Hound* was completely booked out from 7 am until past midday. She also had the unenviable task of getting Jake and Kayla out of bed, fed, dressed, and dropped off at day-care before the roosters even stirred.

So, as I said, it was me, or no one.

While I waited for Mimi to lick her dish clean, I rang Veronique, told her I'd be late and asked her to 'pretty please' open the shop for me. Couldn't get one past her though. She must have picked up on the anxiety in my voice, which meant I ended up filling her in on the real reason for my lateness. After a horrified gasp and a few unladylike expletives, she wished me luck and warned me to be careful.

"It's up to you," she added before I could hang up, "but if you do go ahead and point out the anomalies in Oliver's email to the police, proving he didn't commit suicide, you, Molly and Dana could end up on the murderer's radar. It's like hiring a sky-writer to fly his plane across the sky and leave a ten-foot message out there, saying, 'Come and get me!'

I hung up, my breakfast of toast and cereal swirling in my stomach. What Veronique said was true, but we couldn't just turn our backs on the situation, let someone get away with murder knowing we'd unwittingly contributed to Oliver's death.

Yes, it was risky. Yes, we could virtually be putting our heads on the chopping block while staring into a big bloody cane basket.

Unless we unearthed the murderer first…

"I'm off now, Molly. Stay here as long as you like. The coffee machine is switched on, there's food in the refrigerator and you can sleep it off a bit longer on my bed if you need to. Just don't drive until you're feeling at least eighty-percent compos mentis. Okay?" I sent the white-faced creature scurrying in the direction of my bathroom a quick wave. "And don't forget to text me as soon as you pull up in your driveway to let me know you've arrived home safely."

A grunt that I took for a yes came from behind the bathroom door.

One eye on my watch, I hitched the strap of my knock-off designer brand bag over my left shoulder and clicked leashes onto the collars of both Chloe and a now-smirking Mimi. No way could I trust the sharp-nosed Pomeranian to be well-behaved and 'non-aggressive' in my shop, so I scooped up a small carry-crate to take with me. Chloe spent most days with me, and I couldn't leave Mimi home alone or the inside of my house would look like a bomb crater by the time I returned. So, looked like Mimi the Monster would have to spend the day with me too.

One last grimace at the sound of projectile vomit plastering itself somewhere in my bathroom and I went barreling through the front door. And almost took out a tall willowy blonde who was standing, one arm raised, preparing to knock. *Pussy Willow*, the stripper from *The Pussycat Parlor*.

"Sharon?" Surprised, I took a step back, blinked up at her. "They let you out?"

"Yeah." Her wide grin produced dimples in both cheeks. "The Pigs decided to release me an hour ago. No apology. No poached eggs, pancakes and bacon for breakfast. Just shown the door." She shrugged. "Evidently the real murderer confessed, so the case is now closed."

No, no, no, the case couldn't be closed. I had to reach Lightfoot and tell him what I'd discovered in that fake email.

"*And,*" she said, drawing the word out like she was the animated host in some TV game show, "I have you to thank. They tell me you investigated the gold button I found in the alleyway, discovered it belonged to the show-judge who slept with Petra and when confronted with jail time, he confessed to murdering her." She threw her arms around my neck and hugged me. Or should I say smothered me. The collective smell of strong perfume, stale make-up and cigarette smoke was overwhelming. "I knew I could rely on you, Abi."

I extricated myself from the hug. Peered at my watch. "Um…Sharon, sorry, there's so much I have to tell you, but I'm running late for work." And a trip to the police station, but I didn't think she'd want to hear about that, having just come from there herself.

"That's okay, we'll catch up soon." Sharon peered down at the two dogs at my feet. One standing quietly, ears cocked, head tipped to the side, listening to every word, the other one leaping in the air like a rubber ball on steroids. "Of course, as well as thanking you, I'm here to pick up my little sweetie pie." Her voice changed to a high squeak. "Mimi, darling, Mummy's here to take you home."

As Sharon bent down, the yipping, bouncing, orange whirlwind flew through the air and landed squirming like a hot potato in her arms, tongue attacking every reachable spot on her face, neck, ears and nose.

I flinched. "Um…sorry she's still in her Poo-Bear PJ's," I said, pulling a face and feeling like a neglectful Auntie for sending Sharon's baby home in the same clothes as she arrived in. "I did try to take them off, honest, but the way she reacted, she must have thought I was trying to steal them."

Sharon laughed and kissed Mimi on the nose. "Who's my little girl?

Mimi's my little girl. Who wouldn't let Aunty Abi change her clothes? My little Mimi girl." She peeped at me over the dog's head. "She *does* like getting her own way."

Hmm…*Is that what you call it?*

"But who can resist my teeny weeny sweetums umpy-scrumpy little face?"

Yeah. Right. I looked down at Chloe and Chloe looked up at me. We both rolled our eyes. "Look, Sharon, I really have to go. I'm so late. Maybe we can catch up for a coffee in a couple of days and you can tell me all about your *holiday* in the Big House."

"Yeah, that'd be great. Here, pass me your phone and I'll add my number to your contacts."

I handed her my cell, and while waiting for her to program her number, opened my mouth to tell her about the discrepancies in Oliver's so-called suicide note and how maybe the gold button was a plant, then for some reason I closed my mouth again, without saying a word. The case might be closed to the police, but not to Dana, Molly and me. And until we delved a little deeper into this mystery, we couldn't trust anyone. Even if Sharon had a water-tight alibi for Oliver's time of death. The best alibi possible – she was in a jail.

The moment Sharon returned my phone, I dropped it in my bag, handed Mimi's leash over and closed and locked the front door. One quick glance at my watch told me Veronique would be opening the doors of the shop right now. And I hadn't even left home. Another wave to Sharon and I was backing my car out onto the roadway.

Due to heavy traffic, it took longer than I anticipated to reach the Port Adelaide police station. But fortunately, only two minutes to find a park, assure Chloe I wouldn't be long, lock the car and jostle my way through the front doors.

"I need to talk to Detective Lightfoot," I told the policewoman typing away on the keyboard of her computer. The same indifferent cop we'd encountered the day before.

"He's busy at the moment. Please take a seat."

Must be her standard welcoming spiel.

"I haven't got time to take a seat. I'm late for work."

She glanced up long enough to run an eye over my belligerent body stance and scowling face. "Oh, it's you," she said and went back to her typing.

"Look, it's important that I speak to Detective Inspector Lightfoot. I have more information about the Petra Sullivan case."

"DI Lightfoot wouldn't be interested. The Petra Sullivan case is closed."

"But–"

"He won't see you," she said and looked at me under her eyes. "In fact, he gave me strict instructions he was not to be disturbed." And by the determined expression on her face, he'd also tacked on, '*especially by one of those nosy amateur sleuths.*'

Now what? I stepped away from the desk to allow a homeless guy in 1960 style trousers so encrusted with dirt, so stiff, they could have stood up without the help of legs, and a discolored plaid shirt that wasn't even suitable for mopping up floors, to take my place.

"Someone pinched me bottle." Reeking of cheap booze and something akin to sour bile mixed with even sourer urine, the man leaned his body over the front desk.

"Everyone's busy at the moment. Take a seat, please."

Yep. Standard answer.

I sighed. Bit my bottom lip. I couldn't just up and walk away and not alert the authorities to the anomalies in Oliver's email. Not if it meant a murderer would get away free. The moment Homeless Guy shuffled off to park his stiff pants onto a hard, white plastic chair, I fronted the disinterested policewoman again.

"Look, if I can't see DI Lightfoot, can you please pass on a message to him from me? It's important." When she fired a scowl in my direction, I decided to get my point over quickly before she decided to either arm wrestle me out the door or toss me in an empty cell. Or a not-so-empty one. "Just tell the DI that Oliver Hutchins did *not* write that email. Whoever murdered him wrote it. Oliver corresponded like a cross between a lawyer and a politician and that email could not have been written by him. For a start, there's no way Oliver would make a joke about going to jail. No way."

"Ms. Truelove, I appreciate you wanting justice to be done, but as I said before, the Petra Sullivan case is closed. Leave the investigating to the police. It's our job, not yours. Plus, you'll stay alive a lot longer."

"But you *will* pass on the message?"

She rolled her eyes. "Only if you're out of this building before I count to three, and then, only if the DI's in a good mood when he comes out of his office." She lifted both eyebrows in a scary-chick mode, but I noticed the corners of her lips twitched. "Now, go!"

There was nothing more I could do. I shoved the printed copy of the email with the underlined anomalies at her and then left her to deal with the next person in the queue, a beefy guy with a face full of colorful tats. Seemed as if he had a bone to pick with a parking meter out the front of the building that had supposedly taken his fifty-dollar note and didn't spit out any change.

No wonder the police woman was showing little enthusiasm for her job.

It was now half an hour since Veronique opened the shop, so I scrambled into the van, gave Chloe a liver treat and a kiss on the nose for being such a good girl while waiting, then floored the accelerator. I'd give it until the end of the day, and if I hadn't heard from the DI by then, I'd ring him. And keep ringing until he answered.

As I drove, I couldn't stop thinking about that email. I wasn't keen on Dana's theory that the motive for Oliver's murder was revenge for Petra's death. All the evidence pointed to the same person murdering both victims. But who? Who would want both Petra and Oliver dead? I could sort of understand Petra as she had a ton of enemies, but why kill Oliver as well?

To give the police a reason to close the case.

And they'd succeeded.

Which meant, it was now up to the *Gumshoe Chicks* to keep the investigation ongoing, for Oliver's sake. But where to look first?

I guess the most likely place was in the dog show world. After all, that was both Petra and Oliver's world. And last weekend three of the competitors in the Best in Show line-up had been furious about being cheated out of the Best in Show trophy by Petra and Oliver.

Plus, Petra was strangled with a dog-leash.

A *Chanel* dog-leash.

A leash identical to the designer brand I sold at *Pampered Pooch*. In fact, we were the only pet shop in a hundred-mile radius that handled designer brand leads. I shivered as though icy fingers had brushed up against my warm skin. What if the killer had purchased the murder weapon from my shop? What if I'd handed the leash over to the killer, put his or her credit card through the device, popped the gorgeous leash into one of our luxury tote bags and maybe even waved as he or she sauntered out the shop? First chance I got this morning I'd check all the receipts, see who'd bought a *Chanel* leash from us in the last year. That decided, I let out a sigh that originated from somewhere deep inside my shoes.

What were we getting ourselves into?

Fifteen minutes later, I parked in front of *Pampered Pooch,* undid both Chloe's and my seatbelt and climbed out of the car. Even in my hurry, I couldn't suppress a grin of satisfaction as I checked out the premises. The store was quaint in an old-fashioned way yet colorful and modern. Aunt Tilly smiled at me from the blown-up photo I'd arranged in the middle of the window display. I was sure she'd be looking down from whichever cloud she'd taken over and giving me a thumbs up. *Pampered Pooch* had always been her baby for as long as I could remember. As a kid, I'd spent a good part of every school holiday amongst the dog paraphernalia, helping out and getting pocket money in return.

"There you are." Aunt Tilly's best friend, Veronique, bustled over, a teal scarf tied fashionably around her neck matching her blousy top.

"You okay, Abi? Were you followed? Did the detective listen to you? Is he going to keep the new evidence secret so the murderer doesn't find out?"

I laughed. "Let me just put my bag down and grab a coffee and I'll tell you everything." I looked around. The shop had two customers, a man and woman, clearly doting parents of the regal-looking black and white Shi Tzu nestled in the woman's arms. They were engrossed in the weighty task of choosing a set of booties for their canine-child. "Has the shop been busy?"

"Been a run on the items in the 25% off sale. Moved five of those doggy denim jackets and a couple of sheepskin lined winter coats. Also sold two *Gucci* outfits from the consignment of fashion-wear that arrived yesterday." She grinned. "You should have seen Mrs. Bucket's little Sadie dressed in a *Gucci* sailor suit. Oh, she looked adorable." Veronique rummaged in her back pocket and dragged out her phone. "Here, I took some photos to show you."

By the time I'd finished admiring the twenty-something pictures of Sadie, a miniature poodle posing in the cutest little sailor outfit imaginable, the Shih Tzu and her devoted owners were ready to exchange two hundred-dollars for three lots of foot-wear. A set of Yellow Duckie dog slippers by Barko, a set of Zoomies – pink denim canvas Hi-top 'converse' style running shoes with white laces – and an exquisite set of finely knitted bootees in a fetching lilac shade that complimented the dog's eyes.

"Now!" said Veronique the moment the customers were out the door. "What did DI Lightfoot say about your new evidence?"

"Nothing. He's closed the case and refused to budge out of his office."

"So, whoever murdered Petra and Oliver will get away with it, scot-free."

"No way. We feel responsible for Oliver's death. If we hadn't accused him of strangling Petra and used that planted gold button to get him charged, he'd still be alive."

"You can't blame yourselves. Only one person's responsible for Oliver's death. The monster who pulled the trigger."

"But if the police aren't willing to follow up on that email, then it's up to us to continue with the investigation." I chewed on my bottom lip to deter the lurking tears. "For Oliver." I sniffed, blew out some air. Then I straightened my shoulders. "You know, I have a feeling these murders have links to the dog show world. Both victims are connected. Petra was a competitor and Oliver a show judge. So, I'm going to check our receipts and find out who purchased a *Chanel* dog leash from us over the last twelve months." I thought back to that horror-filled moment when I tripped over Petra's strangled body in the alleyway, and shuddered. "Okay, I wasn't in the head space to squat down and really examine the condition of the murder weapon at the time, but when I think back, the lead used to kill her looked almost new."

An hour, two cups of coffee, and eleven more paying customers later, we had the names of all the people who'd purchased an identical lead to the murder weapon. A dozen in all. But only four connected to both Petra and Oliver, the two victims.

Stephen Channing – the incensed poodle guy, co-owner of *Windswept* Kennels. He was furious with both Petra and Oliver when he found out why Petra's dog beat his standard poodle for Best in Show.

Lady Felicity – whose cocker spaniel *Mein Freund Merry Widow* was a hot tip to win Best in Show under Oliver.

Wild Bill Hooter – working dog group winner and a scary guy who ran a wild-life sanctuary that housed several man-eating crocodiles.

Sharon Bottomly (aka *Pussy Willow*) She didn't like Petra after the woman caused her friend to commit suicide, but as far as we knew, Sharon had no connections with Oliver.

And Luke Brody – my ex-boyfriend and Petra's latest lover. The guy who'd intimated that Petra knew better than to reveal her *assets* to other men.

I shot Veronique a puzzled frown. "When did Luke buy a *Chanel* dog lead? And why?"

"Umm, about a month ago. You were at the warehouse at the time and he told me to keep it quiet as he was buying the leash for your birthday."

A block of ice the size of a golf ball jammed itself between the auricle and ventricle of my heart. "But Luke gave me a bottle of perfume for my birthday. A knock-off he bought from the market."

So, who did he buy the fancy leash for? His new girlfriend, Petra? And did he wrap it around her throat and squeeze the life out of her when she told him she'd already moved on and bedded twenty or thirty new guys since hooking up with him?

13

Six hours later, determined to discuss the names on my new suspect list, I marched back into the kitchen. My two best friends were seated at the table, a steaming cup of coffee and a Dagwood *whatever-could-be-found-in-my-fridge* sandwich in front of them.

"Sooo," I drew the word out until they both looked up. "If we're serious about continuing with this investigation, we need to be more organized. Maybe even take notes."

Munching on their respective sandwiches, Molly nodded while Dana tipped her head to the side.

Guess that meant they both agreed with me.

Loud giggles from the next room indicated Dana's children, Kayla and Jake, plus the three dogs, were being suitably entertained via the zany adventures of Disney's *Puss in Boots*. A DVD I'd just slotted into the player.

Eager to get started before the next distraction, I fossicked around in the drawer next to the dishwasher until I came across a biro that actually worked, plus a pale blue writing pad. The pad, sporting little caricatures of dachshunds along the top of each page, had been a present from Veronique on my last birthday. I'd been saving the gift for a special occasion. Looked like this was it.

"Now," I continued, hauling out a chair and arranging my notepad and biro neatly on the table beside my own cheese and gherkin sandwich, before sitting down. "Are we ready?"

Dana flicked a piece of what looked like ham, or maybe fritz as I couldn't remember having any ham in my fridge, from in between two of her front teeth. "Let's start with the names of the people who bought a dog-leash, identical to the one used to strangle Petra, from your boutique. You said over the phone you'd checked this out."

"Yes, Veronique and I went through all the receipts and settled on five people who hated Petra enough to kill her. And if we find Petra's killer, I think we'll find Oliver's too." I blew on my coffee and took a couple of sips. "Okay, here they are, in no special order. Stephen Channing, Luke Brody, Lady Felicity, Sharon Bottomley aka *Pussy Willow* and Wild Bill Hooter. They each bought a *Chanel* dog-leash from us over the last twelve months, and they all had a grudge against Petra, and, or, Oliver."

"Write Luke's name on top of the list," said Molly, scowling as she leaned back in her chair. "Always did think you were too good for that creep."

I blinked at her. "You never told me that before, Moll. In fact, at the dog show, when Petra announced to everyone within hearing distance that she was sleeping with Luke, you said, 'no way, Luke loves you'."

She shot me a *duh* eyeroll. "How could I say the guy's an asshole whose only interests in life are football and himself, when you were living with him?"

"Um…guess so." I wrote *Luke Brody* in copperplate writing on the top of the blank page. Then I drew a small cartoony stick-figure of Luke with his head buried in a pile of steaming horse manure. "You know, when I told him that Petra was pole dancing at the *Pussycat Parlor*, Luke's face screwed up like a cat's backside. He was so peed-off, he slammed the door behind him."

"That so?" Dana leaned over, relieved me of the biro and notebook, drew an exploding rocket that appeared to be stuck up Luke's posterior, then, evidently pleased with herself nudged both biro and pad across to Molly. By the time the pad came back to me there was also a bull in the picture and the bull was aiming straight at Luke's exploding rear. She winked at me. "Right, next name on the list?"

"Stephen Channing." I smothered a giggle at the embellished artwork as I wrote Poodle-guy's name underneath Luke's. "Now, *this* guy is a serious contender. He has one of the top poodle-breeding kennels in Australia and his standard poodle, *Windswept Fly By Me* was odds-on favorite to win Best in Show last weekend. When he discovered Petra had been sleeping with Oliver in return for awarding her mediocre pug the prized award, he looked ready to rip out Petra's entrails and use them to beat her over the head. Which means, Stephen Channing had a very big bone to pick with *both* victims."

Dana, frown furrowing her forehead as she contemplated this theory, tapped her fingers on the table. "But is the bone big enough to risk going to jail for murder and thereby losing everything he's worked so hard to achieve in the dog show industry?"

"I guess that's for him to know and us to find out."

"Unless we're missing something," mused Molly who had her romance-writer face on. "Was Stephen romantically involved with Petra? Could he have been jealous when he knew she'd slept with Oliver?"

"Molly, the guy bats for the other team."

"Hmmm." She drew the word out and I could see her author brain ticking over as she went through the plots of all the books she'd written so far. And came up empty. But of course, that didn't stump Molly. She just invented a new plot on the run. "What if, one night when Stephen was at the *Pussycat Parlor*, Petra seduced *him*." She hesitated, then must have noticed the *WTF* expressions on our faces and hurried to explain. "You know, after spiking his drink with one of those date-rape drugs you read about in the paper, and then, being a blackmailing badass, she threatened to tell Chi, his partner, that she and Stephen were an item?"

Dana raised one eyebrow. "And what? Stephen decided to shut her up, permanently?"

Molly's expression said, *why not,* as she lifted one shoulder in a shrug.

"Mmm…it's a theory, I guess, but I can't see Chi believing anything detrimental about his beloved Stephen. Especially from someone like Petra."

I pulled the notebook closer, doodled a sketchy skull and crossbones motif in the margin. "Still, it's worth investigating, and as I said before, Stephen is a serious contender for the crime. Hey, I was there. I saw the guy's face when he stormed out of that show-ring and confronted Petra, and wow, if looks could kill, Petra and her little overshot pug would have been incinerated on the spot."

Molly skulled the last of her coffee and stood up, then moved across the room to refresh her cup. "I have a friend of a friend whose been looking to buy a standard poodle puppy. What if we use that as an excuse to drive out to *Windswept Kennels* tomorrow and check Stephen out? Maybe ask a few questions. Check his body language when he answers."

"Excellent idea, Moll. And while you and Dana keep him busy showing off the puppies, maybe I'll get a chance to have a bit of a snoop around."

"Okay, I'll ring Stephen tonight and make an appointment."

"Good." I nodded at Molly before writing the second name on the notepad. "Next we have Lady Felicity. Now, that woman, with all her high-falutin' ways was also ready to strangle Petra when she learned her cocker-spaniel had been cheated out of the Best in Show trophy. Even though it hasn't a brain in its head, her dog really stood out in the final line-up. It was a close call between Stephen's poodle and Lady Felicity's *Mein Freund Merry Widow.*"

"Which means we need to question her too," said Dana.

"Right, now there's only two more suspects on this list. That scruffy, Paul Hogan lookalike, Wild Bill Hooter, with the well-trained border collie that won the working dog group last weekend…"

"The weird guy who has crocodiles on his farm?"

"Yeah, that's him. And then there's my new friend from the *Pussycat Parlor*, Sharon Bottomley aka *Pussy Willow*."

"What was Sharon's relationship with Petra?"

"Definitely not best-friend material." I screwed up my nose. "She told me a friend of hers committed suicide after Petra dumped him in front of all his mates. The poor guy was besotted with the woman and couldn't live without her."

"Wow!"

'Yeah, so I guess Sharon had motive, plus opportunity to kill Petra." I gave a quick shake of my head. "But she couldn't have killed Oliver. The police only released Sharon from jail this morning and Oliver was murdered yesterday."

Two murders...

A cold shiver shimmied up my spine as reality injected my senses with a heart-jolting bump.

What the heck were we getting ourselves into here? By feeling in some way responsible for Oliver's death, the *Gumshoe Chicks* were now chasing a double murderer.

Luke's angry face floated into my mind. His chilling words kept rattling around in my head. *'Petra knows better than that.'*

I gulped. Did that mean one of the murder suspects had a double reason to come after me?

14

"Hold still, darling, while I finish cleaning your ears." As I spoke, Chloe reached around and gave my cheek a soggy lick. I kissed her on the nose. "I know ear-cleaning is not your favorite thing, but we can't have you looking anything but perfect for your visit to *Windswept* kennels. They're like Royalty in the show-dog world."

I'd bathed Chloe in a super new shampoo that smelled like a flower shop, toweled her dry and was now applying the finishing touches to her grooming. Even if she didn't leave the car while we were visiting Stephen and Chi, I couldn't risk having them think my dachshund was in any way inferior to their well-muscled, groomed-to-an-inch-of-their-lives, poodles.

Hmm…now what does that say about me as a potential mother? Would I be one of those soccer-mums who jumped up and down at the side of the playing field yelling praise at my child, the best player on the ground, and pitying other mother's children for being so useless?

Maybe it was just as well my womb was allergic to babies.

Molly had rung Stephen the night before and made arrangement for a visit, using the excuse to check out his pups for a friend who was in the market for a poodle. He said he had two litters of standard poodle pups for us to look at. The first eight weeks old, which meant they wouldn't be ready to leave for another four to six weeks, and one older pup, the last offered for sale in a litter sired by his top stud dog,

Australian Champion Windswept Fly By Me and a dam who not only had her title but had thrown several champions in her previous litter. This pup, Stephen informed her, was for sale at the bargain price of $10,000. She'd barely refrained from advising him he needed to shop more frequently at Aldi's.

At precisely 10 am, the pre-arranged meeting time, I heard Molly and Dana pull up out the front of my house. Through the front window I watched Penelope and Busta leap from their cars and greet each other with happy nose sniffs, tail wags and face licks. Both dogs' coats shone in the weak winter sunlight and I noticed a bright new floral bandana gracing Penelope's neck while Busta wore a dark blue velvet collar studded with diamantes and gold leaf. His Sunday-best.

As my van was the roomiest vehicle and therefore better equipped to carry three dogs, Molly slid the side door open and immediately Busta and Penelope clambered inside. Almost as if it were their second home.

I whistled Chloe, who needed no urging, snaffled my tote-bag, phone, and car keys and trundled behind a bouncing barking dachshund out to meet my friends.

"Child-free day?" I said noting Dana's lack of stains, upchuck and children.

"Yep. Dropped the munchkins off at Peter's mum's house. They'll end up with a sugar-high, so flippin' out there they'll be floating on the ceiling, but, hey, I figure that's easier to deal with than keeping sticky fingers away from perfectly groomed poodle coats. Or dealing with the screams and tantrums caused by returning home without a $10,000 poodle puppy of our own."

Windswept Kennels, set on a ten-acre property, was an hour's drive through the Adelaide hills to a little town called Birdwood. I'd once read in a magazine while waiting at the dentist that when Birdwood was first settled by German/Prussian refugees, it was known as Blumberg. And then when World War Two broke out it was renamed after Sir William Birdwood who commanded the Anzacs at Gallipoli. God knows how I remembered all those details. I guess, the fact that I was waiting for the dentist to yank a tooth made me blank out to what was going to happen and absorb the contents of the magazine instead.

This time of the year, the countryside was a verdant green similar to villages in England. However, in summer, when the rains forgot to fall, it would be brown and dry, more like a bushfire waiting to happen.

An hour later, after letting the dogs out for a tinkle and a stretch at a nearby park, I drove the van under an impressively ornate archway and down a raked gravel driveway, so perfect there must have been someone employed to spend eight hours a day continuously raking. Ahead, lay a number of impressively built kennels, but we decided it best to present ourselves at the house first, so I parked under a gum tree in front of the ranch-style home that looked more suited to a family of ten than a couple of workaholic poodle breeders.

"Didn't realize there was this much money in show dogs." Molly's eyes were wide as she took in the opulence of the spread through the car window.

"I've heard Chi's the guy with the moola and Stephen's the guy with the muscles," Dana told her.

"This your first time?" I asked Molly.

"Never had any reason to come here before. State of the art, isn't it?"

"And I bet a pile of Chi's money has been invested to make it that way." I switched off the ignition and turned to my two co-investigators. "Okay, ladies, here's the plan. Don't be too obvious when asking questions and keep an eye open for clues."

"That's your plan?" Dana rolled her eyes.

"What clues are we supposed to keep an eye out for?" asked Molly.

"I don't know, do I? Anything that shouldn't be there or that looks suspicious." I shrugged. To be honest, I was as completely at sea as Molly. "But if one middle-aged mystery writer like Jessica Fletcher can stroll into any crime scene and spot a clue, surely three intelligent women in their twenties can do the same."

"Don't stress, Moll. You'll know it's a clue when you see it," Dana assured her friend while rubbing Penelope, her anxious-to-get-out-of-the-car greyhound's ears. She fished several treats from her ever-ready family bag and distributed them between Penelope, Chloe and Busta.

"Try to slip in a few questions about Petra and Oliver," I suggested, looking directly at Molly. "But without making Stephen nervous or suspicious."

"Why me?" she wailed. "What will you be doing?"

"I'll be investigating. As soon as you get Stephen totally involved in discussing the puppies, I'll slip away and have a snoop around, see if I can pick up any guilty vibes or evidence that either Petra or Oliver have been on the property lately."

Molly frowned. "And what about Dana?"

"Dana is our anchor person. She's here to do both. Keep Stephen and Chi talking puppies and pedigrees and also keeping her eyes open for clues."

Then, with not an inkling between us, we climbed out of the van and made our way up the pathway to the front door of the house.

It was Chi, Stephen's partner, and supposed lover, who answered our knock. Asian in appearance and the owner of such a sweet smile and personality, I had no idea what he saw in Stephen. They were a perfect example of opposites attract. Where Stephen was coarse and gruff, ready to bite your head off if you disagreed with his opinion, Chi was always there with a friendly smile, off-the-charts fashions and a warm welcome.

"Come in," he said, his dark eyes twinkling. "Stevie's in the kennel house grooming dogs ready for the show tomorrow." A small-boned man, Chi wore a pretty floral apron over iridescent pink trousers and a blousy Hawaiian shirt. He opened the door wider. "Not a good day to be out and about. The wind's colder than frog's legs. How about I make you all a nice hot coffee to warm your bones before checking out the puppies?" He made a production of wiping his hands on the front of his apron. "If you're brave, I'll even let you try out my newly baked cookies."

Newly baked cookies? I think I drooled about then. No wonder the mouthwatering aroma wafting through the house had sent my stomach-juices into begging mode the moment Chi opened the door.

"No, don't worry, we–" Dana began.

"Yes, please," I butted in slapping Dana with a stink-eye glare. No way was I going to say no to cookies that smelt like they'd been baked in Heaven. "Didn't know you were into the culinary arts, Chi."

"I just adore going all girlie in one of my frilly aprons and cooking up a storm in the kitchen." He let out a tinkly laugh that would have done Tinkerbelle proud and shook his head. "And just as well too. If it was left to my Stevie, we'd be living on take-aways and toast." He led the way into the kitchen which could have come straight from a *Home Beautiful* magazine. Shiny whizz-bang appliances dominated, including a fancy built-in coffee machine, a stunning mirror-backed wine fridge and more IT gadgets than a research lab.

After sitting us down on high stools, their seats covered in rich red velvet and facing a hatchway, Chi slipped both hands into yellow-duckie oven mitts, so fluffy and cute, I thought they were wasted as oven mitts. I could see them becoming popular as doggy-toys at the boutique. He opened the oven and removed a tray of what appeared to be chocolate chip cookies with the chocolate melting directly into the cookie and placed them on the counter next to another tray laden with already-cooling cookies. He grabbed three bread and butter plates from the top cupboard and slid two of his masterpieces from the tray onto each plate. "Try these, ladies. They're my favorite whenever Stevie and I visit The Cookie Barn. Walnut and white chocolate." He placed a plate in front of each of us. "This is my first attempt at baking them, so I'd value your opinion."

Walnut and white chocolate cookies. Oh, be still my beating heart.

"Now, any preferences in coffee? My Stevie is a coffee aficionado," he said with a whirl on his canary yellow 'converse' sneakers. "Or should I say he's a coffee snob. Once he was offered a cup of instant at a friend's house and now refuses to go back. So, can I get you an extra-mild to extra-strong latte, a cappuccino with adjustable froth, ground coffee? Your choice."

"Cappuccino for me thanks – with lots of froth." I grinned. This sleuthing business wasn't all bad. And even if I ended up with a sugar high and a cappuccino moustache, it would definitely be worth it.

While Chi programmed two extra mild lattes for Molly and Dana and a cappuccino for me, I bit into the first cookie on my plate and almost went into cardio arrest at the deliciousness. Chi could come and live in my house any day of the week – as long as he brought his cooking paraphernalia, his frilly apron, and his Barista coffee machine with him.

After the second walnut and white-chocolate indulgence had disappeared down my throat, I steeled myself to forget about aping Oliver Twist by asking Chi for one more and get on with the investigation. Pushing back my plate, I drew in a deep breath, contemplated how to be super subtle with my first question…

And before I could open my mouth, Molly broke in. "Chi, do you know anything about Petra Sullivan's murder?"

Both Dana and I gaped at each other, Dana adding a horrified frown in Molly's direction while I kicked her under the table. *Not*-Nancy-Drew must have picked up that maybe she'd been a bit blunt as she quickly added. "Um…it was awful, wasn't it?"

"Oh dear, yes. A horrible way to die. Poor woman." Chi bustled around the kitchen picking up our empty plates and cups and transferring them to the dishwasher as though both the conversation and morning tea were now over. "Of course, Stevie and I didn't know Petra very well. Didn't mix in her circles."

"But you did." Dana evidently decided she may as well continue with Molly's eye watering candor. "I mean, Petra was always either hanging around at the dog shows or competing with her little pug, so you must have come across her quite regularly."

For a moment Chi's dark eyes lost their twinkle as they settled on Dana. And then he appeared to pull himself together as he brushed an imaginary speck of dust off his sleeve and his sweet smile returned. I could see his brawny muscle-bound lover, Stephen, strangling Petra, but not Chi. There was something fundamentally good about this man. And it wasn't just the fact that he was a master cookie-baker.

"Okay, you're right," he admitted with a little shoulder shrug. "We knew her, but neither Stevie nor I took to the woman. Especially after we found out she'd slept with the judge to win Best in Show at the Ladies Kennel-Club event. Makes you wonder how many other times that happened." He dragged out a stool and sat down at the table next to me. "Petra Sullivan wasn't a nice person, but she didn't deserve to die, not like that, strangled in a lonely alley at the back of a strip club."

I mumbled in agreement. After all, I'd been up close and personal in that lonely alley in the early hours of the morning and witnessed the end result of that strangling. And it hadn't been pleasant.

"Stevie and I heard on the news this morning that it was actually the show judge she slept with, Oliver Hutchins, who killed her. They said he confessed, committed suicide and now the case is closed." He shook his head and let out a sigh. "I guess we'll never know what really prompted the man to lash out and kill her. Whole thing seems very sad to me."

To tell Chi the truth or not? If he or Stephen were involved, it would be best to let them continue to think the case was closed. I pushed away from the table. Time to move onto the other member of this twosome and see if he were more forthcoming.

"But Oliver didn't kill Petra."

Motor Mouth Molly was at it again. I stood up, stared fixedly at Molly and then turned to Chi who was frowning.

"But I heard it on the news this morning." He looked confused. "The police said the case was closed."

"Molly gets so involved in her writing she rarely listens to the news and wouldn't have heard the latest." I picked up my bag and stared at the other two until they scrambled to their feet too. "Thank you so much for morning tea, Chi, but we'd better go take a look at these puppies. I'm due back at the boutique at 1.30 to take over from

Veronique. It's her niece's wedding this weekend and she's having something special done to her hair." I waved a hand in the direction of the two cooling trays of cookies. "You know, if ever you get tired of showing poodles, you could always set up a cookie shop. People would flock to buy your cookies." I was gabbling to get his mind off Molly's damning statement. "You could call yourself The Cookie King."

"The Cookie King?" queried Dana, raising one eyebrow. "Surely you can think of something a little more original that that?

"Okay, what about Cookies R Us? Cookie Cutter? Chi's Cookies? Melting Moment Cookies?"

"Mmm…" said Dana heading down the passage toward the front door. "Melting Moments Cookies sounds a bit antiquated. How about an ultra-modern boutique called Cookie Cuisine?"

We left a slightly confused Chi at the door and, following his instructions, hurried through the light rain that had started up while we were inside, over to the last kennel house in the row.

"Molly, darling," said Dana giving our innocent friend a sharp nudge with her elbow as we walked. "To be a good investigator, you need to think before you speak. We don't want anyone outside our circle to know Oliver isn't the murderer. It would put the real murderer on alert. Okay?"

"Sorry." Molly blew out a sigh. "It's just as well I'm not a mystery writer, hey?"

"You're right there, Moll. Although, to be honest, I don't know how you manage to write such sizzling hot romances when you have no man in your life to practice on. And yet, look how far you've come. Your latest novel, *Taming Jessica* jumped into the top 10 on Amazon this month."

We found Stephen, dressed in skin-tight jeans, black boots and a yellow shirt that was artistically done up with one button. All the better to show off his bulging muscles as he lifted a beautifully turned out *Windswept* poodle, kennel-name Orpheus according to the lettering on his collar, off the grooming table and onto the floor. He straightened up and sarcasm burst from his thin lips like vomit. "Oh, so, you've decided to grace us with your company and take a look at the pups at last."

"And a good morning to you too, Stephen," said Dana, hitting him with a scowl. "Your other half – and a much nicer half I might add – was kind enough to tickle our palates with a sample of his incredible cookies."

Stephen rolled his eyes. "That's my Chi for you. Too sweet for his own good. He lets in any motley mob of gypsies that come to the door if he thinks they need fattening up."

Before Dana could reply with a burst of unpleasantness that would get us nowhere, I jumped in, feet first. "I hear you have some baby puppies for sale, Stephen. Molly's friend is in the market for a pup that's suitable for the show-ring."

"Well, duh. Every dog I breed is destined for the show ring. My puppies' pedigrees stretch way back to the 1985 Crufts winner, *Champion Montravia Tommy-Gun* and my top stud dog is a close relation to the 2014 Crufts winner, *American Champion Afterglow Maverick Sabre*." He latched the gate on Orpheus's crate then headed for the doorway. "Well, don't just stand there like wet cakes of soap on a bathroom sink. Come and feast your eyes on perfection. My puppies are all in the playroom at the moment, out of the weather. But I have to warn you, your friend better be prepared to part with a decent chunk of cash if she wants to snatch a *Windswept* puppy from under the noses of all my eager clients."

Molly and Dana surged from the room to follow Stephen as he flounced along a roof-covered pathway with separate kennel-houses built on each side. I held back. Slowed my steps. All the better to poke my head into every kennel house or feed shed or office that we passed on the way to the puppy playroom. I had my eyes peeled for clues, evidence or any other abnormality that might point a finger at the arrogant yellow-shirted poodle-breeder leading the way.

Each separate kennel-house was built to house six poodles. And even from a quick glance through the doorway I could see the dogs had been grouped in various categories. Dogs currently in show-condition, dogs spelling, trainees, puppies, brood bitches and stud dogs. And as well as each room being supplied with a refrigerator, dish-washer, grooming table, built-in cupboards and reverse-cycle air-conditioning, every dog had its very own personal kennel complete with comfortable bed and fresh bedding. If Chi and Stephen didn't lock these kennels at night, they'd wake up in the morning to find the homeless had infiltrated the kennels and were curled up with a bottle of milk in one hand and a dog biscuit in the other.

A little further on, away from the main path and set behind a nicely trimmed hedge, I spotted a separate kennel house, this one larger and a little different to the others. More homey. Less institutionalized. Curtains, featuring little black gamboling poodles on a pale pink background, were hung across each window and the open front door was fitted with one of those special doggy gates where the residents could see what was going on outside, without escaping.

Stephen, Dana and Molly had already disappeared into a large shed that was erupting with distinctive yaps and baby barks, so I checked over my shoulder to make sure Chi hadn't left his kitchen, and then hurried across the lawn. Fascinated, I peered over the barrier. Not a lock-up kennel in sight. Instead, there were soft bean bags and fluffy doggy beds scattered across the floor and along one wall, two well-stuffed couches. A grey-bearded black poodle was curled up asleep on one, and a threesome occupied the other. This must be the Geriatric Ward for old dogs. How sweet. One old dog with a normal poodle cut which was far more comfortable-looking than the out-of-this-world show cuts used in the show-ring, waddled arthritically over to the doggy door and with a toothy grin, licked my hand.

"Hello sweetie," I crooned, scratching him behind the ears. If he'd been a cat he'd have purred. "Just look at you lot. Oh, so comfortably retired." And my estimation of both Chi and Stephen immediately pinged up fifty notches. This proved they really loved and cared for their dogs, even those way past their use-by date.

I leaned over the doggy-door to get a better view of the photos adorning the lime green walls. Photos of these dogs in their heyday, I guessed. Some in the showring being presented with ribbons and trophies, others running free, their coiffed hair blowing back in the breeze like Vogue models as they galloped across the grass.

I leaned forward for a better view and that's when the irresistible smell of cookies wafted across the kennel-house and landed on me.

I lifted my nose, sniffed harder, and like a gundog following a scent, climbed over the barrier and followed my nose to the source. Oh my God. There was a plate of Chi's cookies sitting on a shelf built into one wall, just high enough to be out of reach of the dogs.

Chi had baked cookies for the pensioners and left them to cool off before passing them around. What an amazing Doggy Dad.

Hands clasped behind my back to prevent them from touching, I studied the cookies more closely. They were a little different to the walnut and white chocolate delicacies we'd been fed in the kitchen. These were plainer, with little green bits running through them, and more in the shape of dog biscuits. But they didn't look or smell like any dog biscuit I'd ever come across.

I tried to take a step back, vacate the premises, I *really* did. But the intoxicating aroma of those cookies drew me closer. Hypnotized me. Wouldn't let me go. And then, like it was a programmed robot out of my control, my right hand snaked out and fastened itself around one still-warm cookie, and held on tight. Maybe I could just have a nibble. Just a taste to see what the green things were in Chi's creations. Maybe, I could even entice Chi to make them for me to sell at *Pampered Pooch*.

Then, so Chi wouldn't notice, I nibbled along one side. Very neatly. Very carefully. Mmm…they were different. Unusual. And *so* moreish. Not sure what the green bits were but these dog-cookies were delicious. Maybe Chi didn't count how many he put on the plate and if I finished this one off, he wouldn't realize there was one missing…

And before I knew what had happened, I'd eaten five.

Oh my God. What was Chi going to say when he returned to dispense treats to his pensioners, who were all staring at me in complete disbelief, and discovered there were only three left on the plate. I was a bad *bad* person. A person who deserved to be bitten, dragged around the room like a smelly stuffed toy, and then rolled around and stomped on some more.

I apologized to the disgruntled dogs. Admitted I was lower than road-kill. But after rejecting my apology with hard stares, cold shoulders and upturned noses, they shuffled back to their beds. Not one followed me to the doggy gate to say goodbye. And when I turned around one last time to issue another *'sorry guys'*, I swear the large apricot poodle with the long snooty nose gave me a distinct raspberry.

I'd been gone far too long, so I scooted along the pathway toward the open door of the puppy playroom where I could hear Dana attempting to distract Stephen by asking him multiple questions in regard to pedigrees. Stephen's obsession. He was reeling off names one after the other like reading from an electoral roll.

However, the moment I climbed over the doggy gate into the room, he broke off his lecture in mid-rant. His eyes were frowny-slits as they looked me up and down. "Where the devil have you been?"

"Sorry, I um…followed the sign to the Little Boys and Girls room." I let out a giggle that came from nowhere. Or somewhere I wasn't expecting it to come from. "Hope you don't mind."

I bent to cuddle a gorgeous black poodle puppy with a face as exquisite and fine as Dresden china. Molly and Dana, also patting the puppies, both lifted eyebrows at me in a silent, *'well, did you find anything?'* expression.

Did I find anything? No…

Did I do a bad thing? Heck, yeah!

I shook my head.

There were pups everywhere. Running free, safe in play pens, swinging from hammocks, barking at each other and asking to be picked up and petted. I wanted to get down on my knees and play with them all. Chase balls, roll them over, play tag. I let out another giggle, which ended in a loud hiccup.

What was happening to me? This was a serious investigation and we were here to interrogate the owners of the Windswept kennels. Why couldn't I control my laughter?

Stephen hit me with a frustrated frown. "Well, you should have asked first," he growled and for a moment I didn't know whether he meant I should have asked for permission to giggle or go to the loo. He straightened up, threw out his manly chest, all the better to show off his tan skin and gold medallion. "Chi and I insist on knowing where visitors are at all times," he declared in his I'm-King-of-the-castle voice. "For the security and safety of our dogs we run a very tight ship."

Or was it so no one could go snooping for evidence to incriminate him in a murder?

I giggled again. "Never come across a ship that's been tight *or* loose."

Ignoring me, Stephen placed the coffee-colored puppy he held in his arms on its feet and pointed to another play pen which was shaking with the exuberance of eight baby poodles, all quite a bit younger than the coffee-colored pup. "There's three in this litter for sale." He lifted his chin at Molly. "Was your friend after a dog or bitch?"

"Um…a girl, I think."

That was enough for him to start spouting another pedigree spiel, telling us exactly how many champions and supreme champions the second litter had in their lineage.

"Phew! Is it getting hot in here?" I asked, shrugging out of my heavy fur-lined jacket and dropping it in a pool on the floor. "Still too hot." I started undoing the buttons on my blouse. However, the buttons were playing tricks with me, some jumping off the blouse and refusing to get back on again.

Weird. Very weird.

I giggled and did a little snoopy dance on the spot. Maybe I'd take my underneath tee-shirt off as well.

"*Abi!* What are you *doing*?" Dana snatched my jacket up off the floor while Molly dragged my tee-shirt back down and did up the first two buttons on my blouse. "Have you been getting into someone's happy pills?"

Stephen spun around, pedigrees forgotten, as he stabbed his large sweaty red face smack into mine. He was so close I could see fine grey hairs sprouting out of his nose which made me splutter with glee. Proved he *did* dye his hair black. "Yes, Abigail," he hissed, his voice low, his eyes suddenly cold. "Have you been getting into someone's *happy* pills?"

Whatever was pressing on my funny bone must have thought that was the wittiest line since Rowen Atkinson made his debut in comedy. I almost choked on my giggles.

"Come on, Abi, we're taking you home." Dana elbowed Stephen aside and hooked one arm through mine. "Grab her other arm, Moll, and we'll help her back to the car." She shoved Stephen again as he attempted to grab at the sleeve of my blouse. "Bye, Stephen. We'll get back to you about the pup later. Thanks for your time."

"But she didn't answer my question," Stephen persisted, his voice laced with suspicion. "What has Abi been getting into?"

As Molly and Dana dragged me down the path, past the Geriatric Ward and toward my van, I couldn't stop giggling. Stephen was so funny. He could claim top billing as a comedian if ever Chi opened, *The Cookie King*.

And yet, on the fringes of my brain, where the laughter couldn't reach, I felt fear. Stephen Channing was a big guy with a big attitude. And just before my friends led me away, his eyes, sharp and rock-hard, speared deep into mine.

Chilling me to the bone.

15

It was crowded in the back of the van with the three dogs. Each one convinced I was there specifically to cuddle and play with them.

Body jiggling, I convulsed in uninvited laughter.

Immediately, Chloe's sandpaper tongue washed my face while Busta used my stomach as a trampoline and dear sweet Penelope, a worried expression etched on her face, snuggled her large warm body as close to me as Chloe would allow.

"Hey, Abs, you okay back there?" Dana, who'd asked Molly to take over driving duties so she could strap herself into the passenger seat and check out her phone, tossed the words over her shoulder as we swung out from under the *Windswept Kennels* gateway and onto the bitumen road fronting the property.

"Umph…think so." I pushed Busta off my stomach and Chloe's left leg out of my mouth and gave another giggle.

"Better sit down and fasten your seatbelt."

"In a minute. Dogs seem to be enjoying my company."

"Don't let Busta get too excited," advised Molly glancing at the rear-vision mirror to see what was going on behind. "He's inclined to pee when he gets over-excited."

"We know," Dana and I chanted simultaneously. Many the time we'd had to clean the back of my van with disinfectant when Busta and Jake had been playing a raucous game of 'grab doggo'. And it wasn't caused by the one wearing a diaper.

"Hey," Dana looked up from updating her Facebook page and half-turned in her seat. Her grin was so wide it could be mistaken for the entrance to Luna Park. "I know what's up with you, Abi. You found the guys' marijuana stash, didn't you? Where was it hidden?"

"Marijuana?" I pushed myself up into a sitting position, leaned back against the side of the van and giggled. "I didn't see a marijuana crop growing anywhere."

"Well, what did you get into?"

"Nothing. All I did was check out the kennels and–"

And then it hit me, filtered through the haze in my brain and cracked me over the skull with a sledgehammer. The little green bits in the pensioners' cookies. Chi had laced them with cannabis to give pain relief to the older, arthritic dogs in the retirement shed.

"Oh, God, I ate weed cookies meant for the old dogs." I stared at the roof of the van but all I could see was the disappointed faces of the gray-bearded *Windswept* poodles. Yep, I was lower than road-kill. "Chi must have baked them for his geriatrics to help with their chronic pain. And I went and scoffed them down like the greedy fat pig I am."

"No wonder you can't stop laughing." Dana let out a hoot. "You're full of pot."

"Chi's not our murderer," I mumbled ignoring Dana's levity. "And this proves it. He couldn't kill anyone. He's a good person."

"Just because he loves his dogs enough to flaunt the law and the kennel's reputation doesn't mean he isn't capable of murder."

"Ooh," I said holding onto my head as we went over a bump. "I feel sick."

"Don't worry," soothed Molly. "Once we get you home, I'll make some Chamomile tea for you. It's guaranteed to work wonders."

"Yeah," said Dana with a grin as she leaned over the back seat to pat me on the head as though I was one of the dogs. "Chamomile tea and Panadol. Now that'll help you relax and sleep off all that THC you've ingested."

"Can't." I let out a spluttering giggle that sent the dogs into jump-on-Abi-and-lick-her-face-clean mode again. "I'm needed at the boutique this afternoon. Veronique has a hair appointment at 1.45 and there's no way she can change it at this late date."

"She'll only be gone an hour – two hours tops. I'll see if Peter's mum will hang onto the kids for a little longer. What about you, Molly? Can you help out too?"

"Count me in. I can always complete my daily word-count later tonight. I figure Sebastian and Rebecca need time out anyway. Things are getting a little out of hand in the bedroom."

"Oh, give me strength!" Dana did an exaggerated eye roll.

"I've been thinking," said Molly, eyes glued to the road. "What if *Petra* found out Chi had a marijuana crop and was using it to bake cookies for his dogs? Would that be enough reason for Stephen to kill her so his lover didn't get into trouble?"

"Unlikely," I said settling Chloe onto my lap. "If everyone who grew a few marijuana plants in their backyard for personal use resorted to murder when found out, our jails would be crammed twenty to a cell."

"The idea has merit," said Dana slipping her phone back into the depths of her voluminous bag. "But there'd need to be more to it than that."

"Like what?"

"Well, dah. We're the *Gumshoe Chicks*. It's our job to find out."

"It is? But how?" Going by the wobble in Molly' voice, she didn't sound totally convinced.

"Well, for a start, we have our dogs entered in the dog show on Saturday. Right?"

Molly nodded while I choked on a giggle.

"So, while we're there, not only do we make our dogs beautiful for the presiding judges, we also have to continue with our investigation. There'll be questions to ask, gossip to listen to, and a murderer to track down."

A murderer to track down. I shivered. Cuddled Chloe a little closer.

From inside my tote bag, my phone's ring tone broke through the rising shivers. I dug deep and for some reason found both my purple money purse and an unopened packet of spearmint lifesavers side-splittingly funny.

Before answering, I checked caller ID. "Oh-uh! It's Nathan." I told Molly and Dana with a nervous giggle. This was the first time Nathan had rung since he'd sent Luke on his way, come in for a drink and then watched me fall apart after I'd read Oliver's confession on Tuesday night. "Oh, God, I can't speak to him while I'm like this. I'll have to hang up."

Dana leaned over and snaffled my phone. "Hi Nathan," she said attaching the phone to her ear. "Dana Fox here. Yeah, Pete's fine. Only saying the other day, he must give you a ring, make arrangements to meet up again." She laughed. "Of course, you're always welcome at the guys' fortnightly poker game." She sent me a mischievous wink. "By the way, the um…*person* you rang, Abigail, is currently finding everything in the universe hilariously funny. Evidently mistook a plate full of weed cookies meant for some poor old arthritic dogs for genuine everyday newly baked cookies meant for her. Shocking, hey? Did you still want to speak to her?"

She let out a hoot at whatever Nathan said and passed the phone back to me. "He says that's so sweet and did you save one for him?"

"Nathan?" I pushed Chloe gently away from my face and let out a loud chuckle. "Sorry about that. Can't seem to stop laughing. What's up?"

"I hear you've been stealing marijuana cookies from the mouths of poor old retirees." He let out one of his special bone-melting rich laughs that reminded me of his equally bone-melting kiss at the front door of my house when he left on Tuesday night. Warmth crept into places that didn't need warming. "If you were feeling that stiff and sore, I could have baked some 'special' cookies for you myself. I have the recipe here in the top drawer of my desk. Given to me by a grateful client who got himself smashed up by a muscle-bound thug last year because he wouldn't pay protection money. I staked-out and videoed the same muscle-bound thug beating up another victim and he was charged and incarcerated. My client thought I might need some tasty painkillers for when said thug gets out of jail."

I groaned. And then giggled. "Sounds like they'd come in handy in your line of work."

"Yes." He cleared his throat. Was he nervous? Yikes! That made two of us. "Anyway," he went on, "I rang to see if you'd like to come out with me on Saturday night."

"Saturday night?" That's what the guy said. Why was I repeating it? I took a breath and started giggling again. Half nerves. Half whatever.

"A mate of mine is competing in the World Cup Showjumping Championships at the Royal Adelaide Showgrounds. His horse, *Westward Way Anker*, has a top chance of winning the event and if he does, he could represent Australia in the World Cup finals to be held in Germany later this year. Mike sent me a couple of tickets and I thought you might like to tag along with me."

So, it wasn't a date at a fancy restaurant with six courses and romantic music playing in the background like I'd imagined. "Um…didn't know you were interested in horses."

"Lots you don't know about me, Abigail Truelove." His voice grew warmer, more chocolatey, more intimate. "And here's a chance to learn of my many amazing attributes."

I laughed. "Of which modesty isn't one of them."

"Does that mean you'll come?"

"Well…"

"How about this – if you accompany me to this event, I promise to divulge five fascinating details about me that you don't already know."

I let out a burst of uncontrolled giggling. "Hey, how can I resist an opportunity like that?"

"It's the opportunity of a lifetime."

Once I tamed another burst of laughter, I cleared my throat before answering. "Okay, I'd love to go. Next to dogs, horses are my favorite animal."

"Great. I'll pick you up around 7.30 Saturday night. Okay?"

"Can't wait."

"Oh, yeah, and one more thing. I did an online search on your ex and found his previous girlfriend put a restraining order on him"

"Why?"

"He wouldn't accept that she'd broken up with him and kept coming around to her house, stalking her, abusing her and sending malicious texts."

I choked back an unwanted giggle that was meant to be a gasp. "And did the restraining order work?"

"Don't know, but if Luke comes near your house again, don't let him in. Lock the doors and either ring the police, or me."

Icy shivers skittled up both arms and settled in my throat like a wad of stale chewing gum.

Luke had trouble letting go of his previous girlfriend?

How did I not know that?

16

Around lunch time the following day, the *Pampered Pooch* was invaded by two determined adults, two giggling children, a regal looking greyhound and a boisterous fox terrier.

"What's up, guys?" By the expression on my friends' faces, they had news to impart.

"We're off to see Wild Bill Hooter," declared Dana, tightening the straps to keep Jake in his stroller. Last time her stubborn son was in the shop he'd declared one of the toys on display his own, refusing to let go. Cost Dana $80 for a *Chanel* Buzzy Bee. "Thought we'd better check first to see if you'd like to tag along."

"The Crocodile Dundee guy with the champion border collie?"

Molly nodded. "I heard via the grapevine that he had a grudge larger than the National debt against our late show judge, Oliver Hutchins."

"Interesting."

Molly nodded again, rolling her eyes to emphasize the point. "He almost flipped when he found out Oliver slept with Petra in return for her Best in Show win last weekend."

"I know, I was there, remember. He even spat at her."

Dana shoved Jake's favorite toy, Doggo, into his outstretched hands while waving a warning finger at Kayla who was currently on tip-toe reaching up to examine a set of exquisite flowery dog pajamas displayed on the back of a miniature poodle dummy. The pajamas had a $200 price tag. "I've heard Hooter's turned his property into some sort of wild life sanctuary," she said, her eyes never leaving Kayla. "You know, kangaroos, koalas, dingo, emu."

Molly nodded. "*And* snakes. *And* crocodiles."

"Yikes!" I took a step back. "Do we *really* want to go see this guy? What if we stumble across a half-eaten body in the crocodile pen?"

"According to my sources, which are very reliable I might add–"

Dana gave a hoot. "Your hairdresser and blabbermouth, Suzy Randall, reliable? "Next you'll be telling me Peter Pan runs an adult shop in the local mall."

"Bill Hooter *does* have a man-eating crocodile on his property." Molly poked her tongue out in retaliation, before continuing. "It's called Jaws."

"Naturally."

Molly let that one go. "Story is, five years ago Jaws dragged this bad guy who was on the run after murdering his wife and three kids, into a creek and proceeded to chomp off several vital pieces of the guy's anatomy. Of course, some people wanted the croc shot, but according to Hooter, Jaws should have received a medal for his service to the community."

"What happened?"

"Hooter ended up saving Jaws from a lawman's rifle on the condition the vet removed all the croc's teeth."

"You're kidding me…"

"Nope. That's the story. And since then, he's had five other crocs transferred to his luxury crocodile enclosure. So, do we *really* want to go out there?"

Dana shook her head. "Molly, darling, you are so naïve. People tell you these bizarre stories just to get a reaction."

Having rubbed shoulder with Wild Bill at the shows I wasn't so quick to dismiss Molly's story as unbelievable. I shuddered and then decided to change the subject. "Any idea why he hated Oliver so much?"

"No, sorry," said Molly. "The grapevine didn't have a clue. Although one little old guy who shows a Welsh Corgi in the Working Dog group, seemed to think it might have something to do with Hooter's wife. She left him for some guy a couple of years ago and Welsh Corgi guy thinks it might have been Oliver Hutchins. Only speculation, of course, but I thought it worth following up."

"I guess if Oliver could stoop low enough to elicit sex in return for giving Petra a win, he was also capable of sleeping with a married woman." I glanced across at Veronique who'd been listening with one ear cocked. "You okay to handle the shop for a couple of hours, Ronnie?"

"Go for it. As long as you keep me up to date on what's happening. This is like reading a gripping murder mystery and not being able to cheat by flicking through the pages to find out what happens next."

I grinned across at her. "Hey, once this is all over, you can take a few days off, go read a book that you *can* flick through, visit your sister in Melbourne, whatever, to make up for all the extra work you've done this week."

I finished arranging a set of newly arrived porcelain dog statues onto a prominent shelf at the front of the store and then bent to gather my tote-bag from under the front counter. The speculation that Bill Hooter's wife might have been involved with Oliver was definitely a clue worth investigating.

Once again, due to the larger interior, we all bundled into my big white van. Dogs in the rear alongside Jake's stroller, children strapped into the back seats in their capsules, Molly, Dana and me in the front.

It was a three-quarter hour drive to *Oz Park*, Bill Hooter's sanctuary and farm. The paddocks each side of the rutted path to his house grazed sheep and cattle, goats and even a family of llamas. Jake and Kayla were pointing, laughing and chattering in the back with each new discovery.

As I pulled into the car park marked for visitors, Dana said, "Remember, the reason we're here is to buy goat's milk for Penelope. We'll say she's become allergic to cow's milk and the vet suggested goat's milk. Right?"

"That's okay to use as an excuse," said Molly peering nervously through the window at the large sign declaring, 'DO NOT ENTER – MAN EATING CROCODILES INSIDE THIS ENCLOSURE'. "But the thing is…" She cleared her throat. "We don't know much about this Hooter guy and we're here to question him about Petra and Oliver's murder. What if he *is* the murderer? We could end up behind that fence as crocodile snacks."

"Hey, no worries, it's broad daylight and there's three of us and only one of him." Dana's voice didn't quite match the confidence in her words.

Still behind the wheel and also not wanting to end up as a crocodile bait, I was debating whether to undo my seatbelt and get out or wind up the windows, lock the car doors and slam my foot down on the accelerator.

"Want to go wee-wee, Mummy."

Dana sighed as she looked over her shoulder at Kayla who was busy undoing the straps on both hers and Jake's car seats. "Are you sure, darling?"

Kayla's answer was to cross her little legs and jig up and down on the seat.

Jake grinned and copied his sister's jigging. "Me! Me! Me!"

Another much smaller sign on the other side of the carpark pointed to a small red brick toilet block, so Dana opened the car door and stepped out. "Come on *Gumshoe Chicks*, since when did a few motley crocodiles deter us?"

"Since I read the words, 'do not enter, man-eating crocodiles behind this fence," answered Molly, not moving.

Dana lifted Jake out of the car and closed the door after Kayla. "They're probably all tame. Otherwise, how could Hooter get into their enclosure to feed them?"

"Maybe, whenever the crocodiles look hungry, he just tosses people he doesn't like over the fence to pacify them and doesn't actually go inside himself."

"Molly, come on, snap out of it. How many crocodile deaths have been reported over the news in the last year? None."

"And how many people were reported missing in the last year and never found?"

Molly had a point there. Maybe we hadn't thought this visit through carefully enough. I frowned at the electrically charged enclosure housing Hooter's prehistoric carnivores and tossed up whether to get out of the car or prepare to take off the moment Dana and the munchkins returned from their toilet break.

"Hurry, Mummy. Phuleez."

Dana picked up Jake, grabbed Kayla's hand and set off toward the toilet block at a jog. "We're here to investigate," she yelled over her shoulder. "So, can you please get Jake's stroller out of the car, unfold it and be ready to follow our plan as soon as I sort these two out?"

I looked at Molly. Molly looked at me. And we both let out a deep sigh.

Dana had spoken.

Still staring anxiously at the galvanized wire fence behind which we could see a large artificial waterway surrounded by low scrub, but thankfully no reptile movement, Molly and I eased ourselves out of the van, set Jake's stroller up and checked the surroundings. Behind a scraggly hedge at the end of the driveway, I could see a rambling Colonial-style cottage. Native Australian plants and bushes jostled for superiority across the front, wisps of smoke rose lazily from one of the chimneys and two fully grown kangaroos grazed on the lawn, ears flicking contentedly.

Molly pointed to a large Eucalyptus tree at the end of the carpark. "Hey, look, there's a koala with her baby. So cute."

I followed her finger and smiled at the chunky-faced koala watching us from half-way up the tree, a baby koala's arms clinging tenaciously to her back. If I was Mummy Koala, I'd be grabbing baby and shifting house. Pronto. Couldn't she read the warning sign in front of the croc enclosure?

"G'day there ladies. What can I do for ya?" Bill Hooter, dressed in moleskin trousers, a checkered shirt, suede fringed vest and a battered bushman's hat, waved and called out as he exited the front door of the cottage and strolled toward us. Not only did the two lawn-eating kangaroos and half a dozen well-trained border collies follow him, but ambling along beside the man, tethered to him by a hunk of rope, was a crocodile the size of a small bus.

I swear my jaw hit the pavement as I let out a gasp of horror and for every step Hooter and his little gang took towards me, I took one step back. Molly didn't move. Looked like she'd been nailed to the spot.

Behind me, I could hear our dogs' noisy, *g'day*, as they viewed the oncoming posse from inside the car.

"Hey, no need to get your knickers in a knot, ladies. This ol' boy won't hurt ya. He's got no teeth. See?" He let go a loud guffaw, took off his hat, scratched at his long straggly locks and replaced his hat at a jauntier angle.

No teeth? Ohmygod! The critter eyeing me off like I was a juicy piece of steak must be the infamous *Jaws*. The man-eater, who was only alive because a vet was forced to remove his teeth.

I pointed a shaky finger in the direction of the scaly monstrosity. "But-but-but–"

"Oh, hi there, Mr. Hooter. Glad you're home." It was Dana back from watering her kids.

"Call me Bill." He tipped his hat to her. "Don't I know you three ladies?"

"Yes, I'm Dana and these are my two friends, Molly and Abigail. Like you, we're also into showing our dogs."

He smiled, nodded his head. "Aah, of course. That's where I've seen you."

"Quite a family you have there, Bill." As Dana strode past me, eyes on the strange mixture of creatures at the man's feet, she poked me a sneaky elbow to the ribs. Probably to remind me *why* we were there. "We're after a couple of liters of goat's milk for Penelope, my greyhound. She's developed an allergy to cow's milk and I was told you sell the best goat's milk in the district."

"Sure do."

"Funny doggy!" Jake's eyes lit up and his little fat legs carried him forward out of Dana's reach as he ran straight for the croc who looked to be sizing us all up. Likely wondering which one of us would be the tastiest.

"Nooo, Jakey!" I yelled and threw myself between the eager toddler and the large scaly one feeling a sharp pain in my left knee as I hit the ground. "Don't touch! Not a doggie! Nasty croc bites!"

"Strewth!" As he gawked down at me lying prostrate in the dirt, mere inches from the giant crocodile's open mouth, I could see the remains of the man's breakfast, egg and toast, hiding amongst the few intrusive grey hairs of his beard. "You practicing some special Corroboree dance?"

"Mmmm…" I spat out what tasted like a lump of bird droppings while watching Dana swing Jake in the air before transferring him to the relative safety of his stroller.

"It's alright for the little tacka to pat him. He's quite tame." Bill reached down and ruffled the scales on the crocodile's head. Jaws toothless grin widened, and he rubbed up against Bill's leg like a dog. "Hey, my two grandkids come 'ere every Sunday and play with 'im. Jaws loves 'em. Lets 'em crawl all over 'im." He blew out a sigh. "Very misunderstood creatures are crocs."

"For a good reason," I growled, pushing myself off the ground and backing away from the still-open mouth. "Crocodiles eat people."

"Only if the stupid galahs invade the croc's territory." Bill shook his head and sniffed. "Crocs have rights too, ya know."

Molly, who'd been silent until now let out a squawk as one of the kangaroos butted her in the chest with its head.

"Rita," growled Bill. "Wadda I keep tellin' ya? If ya wanna ask the lady for a scratch behind the ears, you gotta be polite. Not pushy."

"Oh, look, she has a baby." Molly's face lit up as she smiled down at the joey's head poking timidly out from its mother's pouch. "Will she let me pat her baby?"

"Give her a scratch behind the ears and Rita'll be your friend for life."

Molly reached up, gave the Mummy kangaroo a tentative rub behind one pricked ear but as soon as her hand went down near the baby joey, it disappeared back inside its mother's pouch.

"Before I collect your goat's milk, the two ankle-biters might like to take a look at our petting zoo."

Bill bent down on a level with the two children. Jake, who'd been struggling to unfasten the straps keeping him imprisoned in his stroller, stopped squirming and regarded the large bushman with a serious expression, while Kayla peeped out from behind Dana's legs.

"How about I show you my petting-zoo? Lots of cuddly baby animals for you to pat there." He returned Jake's serious gaze with one of his own and spoke to him man-to-man. "What do ya say, cowboy? Wanna pat a baby goat?"

Jake shook his head and pointed at the giant croc on the end of the rope. "Pat Doggo?"

"No patting Doggo," put in Dana quickly. "But we'd love to see your petting zoo, Bill."

He stood up, shook dried mud off his scuffed RM William boots and straightened his battered Akubra. "Come on then, follow me. We can even say howdy to Glad and Dave, a couple of cheeky wombats that usually drop in for a visit and a bite to eat around this time of the day."

Oz Park was a sanctuary for all things great and small. On the way to the petting zoo we passed a family of llamas, all contentedly grazing on the winter grass, two snakes called Billy and Bongo who were fast asleep in their room-sized terrarium, the two cheeky wombats looking for treats and a herd of Shetland ponies eager for apple and carrot scraps.

Only an hour from the city and we could have been transported into another world. A kind world where rescued animals were given another chance at life.

Bill's petting zoo, as he'd promised, was a haven for baby animals. Like Gonzo the six-week old goat who followed Jake around like his shadow, occasionally butting him in the rear so he fell over laughing. And Betty the baby joey who'd lost her mother in a hit and run six weeks ago and needed to be fed a bottle every four hours. Today, this was Kayla's job and the look on the little girl's face as she held the bottle to Betty's mouth was priceless.

"Still want that goat's milk?" Bill tugged on the rope tied around Jaw's neck to bring him to heel, then turned to Dana, one eyebrow cocked. "Or…is it information ya really after?"

Dana's voice was cagey. "Information?"

"I have access to the show-grapevine too, ya know, and I heard you three lady sleuths have been pokin' around and askin' questions about Petra and Oliver's murder." He blew out a snort that ended in a guffaw. "Also heard ya got Stevie Channing's knickers caught up in his privates a couple of days ago." He flicked a grin at each of us in turn. "Tell me, which one of ya scoffed the marijuana cookies? Would have liked to have been a fly on the wall when that happened."

I raised one finger in acknowledgement. "Believe me, when I say, Stephen was in such a temper at the time, if you *had* been a fly, you'd have been splattered all over that wall."

He laughed and then, his expression turning serious, tipped his head to the side. "You think I had something to do with Oliver's death, don't you?"

"Well…" I screwed up my nose. Although rough in appearance, this man's eyes were kind and after experiencing his gentleness with animals, I figured the only way Bill Hooter would get violent was if someone hurt one of his animals.

And yet?

"It did cross our minds," confessed Dana.

"We heard about your wife," Molly added, her voice soft.

"My wife…" Bill's fingers caressed the ears of the closest dog as he spoke, his thoughts evidently elsewhere. Finally, he snapped to attention and faced us. "You're right, ladies, I couldn't stand Oliver Hutchins."

Molly touched him on the arm. He'd got to her too. "If you don't want to talk about it, Bill, that's fine."

He drew in a deep breath and let it out slowly. "Oliver Hutchins, the show judge, cheated with my wife, but contrary to what the gossip-mill says that if Oliver ever stepped foot on my property, I'd feed him to the crocodiles, I honestly wouldn't give him the time of day. And I certainly wouldn't risk jail time by killing the prissy little man. As far as I'm concerned, I'm well shot of Hanna, my ex-wife. Ya see, Oliver hadn't been the first, and he certainly won't be the last. Now we're divorced and I don't have to put up with her moods or her wandering sexual appetite anymore. Instead, I have me critters."

His smile lit up his craggy face and, in that moment, I knew for certain, Wild Bill Hooter was not our murderer.

"Hey, animals might occasionally take a chunk outta ya," he declared, looking like he was ready to get up on his soap box, "but unlike cheating wives, ya know where ya stand with 'em."

And that's when Jake fell into the water trough and all conversation regarding sexual appetites and bloody murder were temporarily put on hold.

17

It was Saturday morning. And like a timid lady-in-waiting, the weak winter sun struggled to break through the dark clouds. It was there, but as I stood by the gate ready to enter the show ring for the second time that day, the dark clouds and the chilly wind were definitely winning the battle.

I bent to run a hand along Chloe's smooth coat, glad I'd chosen jeans and a bright traffic cone orange jumper to wear instead of my denim skirt and long boots. Much easier to bend and run and without the added stress of panties going on display. Not to mention the wind blowing up my skirt and freezing my nether regions.

The grass in the show ring was mowed to within an inch of its life, prepared with loving care by the important grounds-men and maintenance staff. Around me, the cold air seemed to be alive with the low-pitched voices of waiting competitors and the shrill yaps of belligerent small dogs informing the world they'd been Rottweilers and German Shepherds in a previous life.

A regular Saturday afternoon dog show.

"No pressure, darling," I told Chloe who gazed up at me with those big brown almond-shaped dachshund eyes that have continued to melt hearts for centuries. "It's only a game. We win some we lose some. As long as we have a good day out. Okay?"

Her strong whip-like tail agreed with me.

Following behind the four other standard smooth dachshunds who'd also won their prospective classes, I stepped into the show ring, head up, shoulders straight and a smile on my face. Hey, showing your dog is supposed to be fun, isn't it? Otherwise, why do it? Chloe, looking a million dollars, trotted along beside me, forelegs reaching well-forward. With her shiny black and tan coat, her deep chest, her bold and confident head carriage and alert facial expression, she was always a winner in my books.

The hound judge for the day, a stout middle-aged lady with a bold confident head carriage, not unlike the dachshunds presenting in front of her, lifted her nose a little higher as she surveyed the five dogs gaiting around the ring.

As I brought Chloe to a halt and kneeled down on the grass to set her up for the judge's inspection, I spotted my best friend, Molly. She was leaning over the fence watching us. Her grin and upturned thumb told me she thought we had it in the bag. I smiled back at her.

That's when I noticed Stephen Channing, his face so granite-hard it would take a lightning strike to make a dent, striding towards her, body bristling with pent-up anger. He stopped beside Molly and I could see him talking to her, arms waving and face mere inches from hers. Why do some men do that to women? Get into their space? It's as though they want to hit out at us, know it's against the law, so breathe all their anger into our face instead. Anyway, whatever he was saying had Molly shrinking into her oversized pink cable knit sweater. Her recoiling body language and white face said she'd rather be at home in the safety of her writing cave with only her computer, soft music, and the sexual antics of Sebastian and Rebecca to deal with. Not here in real life, facing a garishly dressed male with temper-tantrum issues.

I shot to my feet all set to bolt across the show-ring to get between them, but before I could move, a whirlwind named Dana appeared from nowhere and had Stephen in what looked like a very painful armlock. How she managed to incapacitate a guy almost twice her size, I don't know, but I'm guessing the Judo classes she somehow fits into her busy schedule had quite a bit to do with it.

"Time to channel all that testosterone into grooming your dogs, Stephen," she growled. "Or I might have to break your arm." Her voice traveled across the ring. Even the judge looked up from assessing the dogs, pushed her chin forward and tilted her head to one side, all the better to see and hear the ensuing drama.

The moment Stephen wailed 'enough', Dana let him go and after he'd backed off, she threw a comforting arm around Molly and guided her across to the opposite side of the ring. She glanced at me as she passed and lifted one thumb in the air as if to say, it's okay, get back to showing Chloe.

Satisfied Molly was in good hands, I knelt down on the grass again and set Chloe up for the judge. Neck arched, legs square, tail straight. From the corner of my eye I watched Stephen, red-faced, being led away by little Chi, his partner, and by the smaller man's body language, he was chewing Stephen out, big time.

Although exhibited by a handler whose mind wasn't entirely on the job, Chloe still won Best Dachshund bitch, which meant she stayed in the ring while the other contestants filed out and the winner of Best Dachshund dog swaggered back in. He was a fine specimen with a look-at-me presence, but it took no more than five minutes for the lady judge to proclaim Chloe, *Tempestuous Dawn*, Best of Breed.

"What was that all about with Stephen?" I asked, hurrying over to my friends as soon as I left the ring, blue ribbon dangling from one hand. "Was he threatening you, Molly?"

Molly gave a hangdog shrug. "He accused me of lying about knowing a friend who wanted to buy a poodle pup. Of wasting his time and spying on his kennels. Couldn't really deny it, could I?"

Dana sent me the stink-eye.

"I know, I know," I said, palms up before she could start on me. I'd spent Thursday afternoon giggling, drinking Chamomile tea, sleeping and coming down from the high induced by snacking on Chi's delicious weed cookies. "If I hadn't got myself full of dope and stuffed things up, he wouldn't have known I was checking out his kennels while you and Dana were distracting him with the puppies."

"But," Dana drew the word out, rolled it around in her mouth as though she was tasting it. "The fact that he *is* so all fired-up, maybe means he *does* have something to hide."

"Yeah, that they love their dogs so much they're willing to risk their reputation by attempting to make the oldies lives pain-free."

Dana shook her head. "You're delusional, Abi. Chi maybe, but there's more to it with Stephen."

It was time for Dana to collect Penelope from her crate and warm her up in readiness for the Open Greyhound Bitch class in the ring I'd just vacated. As it was almost time for Molly's class in another ring, they went off together to prepare their dogs. Chloe was still a little jazzed from showing off in the ring, so I walked her around the grounds until she settled, then hefted her under one arm and carried her back to her playpen.

Inside the playpen, Chloe's thick tartan blanket was spread on the ground together with a comfortable fluffy bed and her two favorite toys. Dora Ducky and Sammy the Caterpillar. I popped Chloe inside the pen and dressed her in her warm cerulean blue sheepskin-lined dog rug, rewarded her with two liver treats, made sure her water dish was topped up and then, knowing she was comfy, collapsed my own over-active body into a bright blue (same color as Chloe's rug) canvas fold-up chair. I let out a long, drawn-out breath and stretched both legs in front of me. This was the life. Out in the fresh air, surrounded by dogs, plus a mystery date with my new love-interest, Nathan, to look forward to tonight.

In the ring close by, half a dozen bubbly miniature schnauzers were parading their stuff, so I snaffled a chocolate bar from my bag and settled down to watch.

I'd been relaxing in my chair, enjoying the atmosphere for at least ten minutes when I spotted Stephen again. Decked out in his knock-em-dead showring attire comprising of poison-purple pants, silver vest and emerald avocado-green silk shirt, he was entering Ring 3 with a bright-eyed jet-black standard poodle puppy on the end of the lead. *Windswept Kennels* certainly bred star-studded stock.

I clambered to my feet. With Stephen in the ring, flaunting his muscles and eye-catching outfit at the presiding judge, Chi was on his own. The little man stood beside their rainbow-colored show bus adding finishing touches to the megastar of their team, *Supreme Champion Windswept Fly By Me*, the dog Stephen would be showing later on in the Open class.

Now was a good time to slink across the ground like a very sorry lizard and apologize to Chi for stealing his weed cookies.

"I won't be long, Chloe," I said noting she'd settled on her bed, head on her front paws, bright eyes on the busy goings-on around her.

She flicked me a perfunctory, go-ahead-I'm-happy-snuggled-up-here chin lift, so I dug up my best smile and headed in the direction of the *Windswept* bus. The sooner I got this apology off my chest, the better. After all, Chi had been kind enough to offer Molly, Dana and me cookies when we arrived. There was no need for him to ask us in and feed us, he was just a good guy, and yet I'd responded to his kindness by stealing the cookies meant for his retirees.

Yep, I was definitely lower than road-kill.

"Chi, I know you're angry–" I began coming up behind him.

He spun around, saw who I was and his ready smile slid off his face. "Angry? Try furious. Or incensed. Or maybe even ready to…"

He stopped himself and shook his head, then turned to the poodle standing at attention on the grooming table beside him and went back to teasing the dog's top knot. Chi's body language said I wasn't there, I was completely invisible, he wasn't going to acknowledge me.

I let out a sigh. This wasn't going well. "Look, I'm really sorry, Chi. That's why I'm here, to apologize to you. I know I shouldn't have gone into the kennel house without permission, or eaten your dogs' treats…"

"Humph!"

"But I actually blame *you* for what happened."

That got his attention. Comb in hand, he swiveled around to face me, deep wrinkles of surprise creasing his forehead. "Me? You blame me? What are you talking about?"

"Well, if you weren't such a fantastic cook, it wouldn't have happened. I succumbed to your chocolate chip cookies when you served them in the kitchen, so naturally, when I smelt the fresh dog treats in the kennel house – not knowing they were marijuana cookies baked specially to relieve the arthritic pain in your old dogs – I couldn't resist them. I tried. Honestly. But when that heavenly aroma circled my nose, my stomach took over. Couldn't help myself. And of course, after eating one, how was I supposed to stop? So, yeah, I blame you. It was all your fault."

For a moment the corners of Chi's lips twitched slightly and then he became serious again. He frowned. "And how much are you going to demand from us to keep this from the show authorities?"

"Whaaat?"

He went on teasing the dog's topknot without looking at me. "Because you stuck your nose, or your greedy mouth, where it wasn't wanted, Stephen's put his foot down. Says I can't bake any more special cookies. And that means poor little Gretel, arthritis in every joint, and Horace with his bad hip, will be the losers. And even Big Bobby, with his arthritic shoulder will go back to hobbling around instead of playing with his squeaky caterpillar toy." Chi's voice broke as he turned damp eyes on me. "He said it has to stop. And you know why? Because you're the third person to blackmail us."

"Blackmail? Chi, what are you talking about? I came over to apologize for depriving your oldies of their medicinal treats, not to-"

"First Petra blackmailed us and then that weasel of a judge who slept with her – and now, *you*." Chi stiffened beside me. He'd spotted Stephen barreling towards us, his black puppy straining to keep up. "You'd better go."

"You've got it all wrong, Chi," I told him, horrified he'd think so little of me.

"Get lost, before Stevie gets here. My honey's a sweet little pussycat most of the time but when he's wronged, he turns into a snarling tiger."

One look at Stevie, the *snarling tiger,* and I decided Chi was right. Time to get the hell out of Dodge. This pussycat had his claws bared, sharpened to points, and ready to rip flesh.

Mine…

I found Dana gaiting Penelope around the ring in her Best of Breed class. She was up against a black and white male greyhound, but in my eyes, Penelope stood out like the Princess she was, and the other dog didn't compare. I joined Molly at the rails to cheer them on.

"If they win this, they'll be in the Hound Group line-up with you." Molly leaned further over the fence, eyeing off the two dogs. "And Penelope hasn't put a foot wrong."

"When does she ever? That dog is a model of good behavior and manners at all times."

"Wish it would rub off on Busta. Naughty little tyke blew it in his class. Wouldn't stop jumping up on my leg trying to get hold of the treat in my pocket."

I laughed. "You know he's the World's Worst Scavenger and yet you take food into the ring. What did you expect?"

At that moment, the hound judge, nose still high in the air, presented Penelope with the Best in Breed sash and both Molly and I pushed aside all thoughts of blackmail and angry poodle breeders and let out a cheer.

Penelope turned her regal head toward us and smiled that special gentle loving smile. The one she reserved for Jake, Kayla, and her very own cheer squad. The moment they came out of the ring she and Dana headed towards us. Penelope eager for her victory cuddles.

Naturally Petra's murder and Oliver's suicide confession were the talk of the show. Everywhere we went we could hear snatches of conversation and speculation.

In the queue, waiting to order three hot dogs with ketchup plus mustard for our lunch, the woman behind me, an elderly lady with a face that had seen far too much sun over the years was chatting to her friend, another sixty-something lady with a face equally scrunched up and weathered like an over-used brown paper bag.

"If the judge, Oliver Hutchins hadn't confessed to killing Petra, I'd have laid a bet on Lady Felicity being the murderer," said Brown Paper Bag number one.

Lady Felicity?

Instantly my ears pricked up and wiggled and strained to hear more.

"I'd have put a few dollars on that outcome myself," agreed Paper Bag number two waving a half-eaten donut around to emphasize the point. "Poor Felicity never got over being in love with Oliver. Did you know, at one stage they were engaged?"

"I heard about that. Any idea why they split up?"

"Nah, it was all hush-hush at the time." Paper-bag number two shrugged, swallowed a mouthful of donut. "Anyway, Felicity probably thought she had a chance to get back with Oliver when he came here for the show. And then he up and made a laughingstock of himself by sleeping with the slut of the show world, Petra Sullivan." She selected another tasty looking chocolate-creme donut from her bag and licked at the icing before continuing. "*And* not content with that absurdity, he made a bigger fool of himself by awarding Petra's dreary pug, *Princess Sauvignon of Glenville*, the Best in Show trophy." She wriggled her false teeth around in her mouth a little, probably to dislodge a crumb from the last donut. "When everyone in the show world knows my exquisite *Emmeline* is far superior to that overshot pygmy of Petra's."

I couldn't help feeling sorry for Petra's pug. No one had a good word for the poor little tyke. She'd been called dreary, undershot, overshot, pathetic and now a pygmy. And with Petra dead, she didn't even have an owner. I made up my mind to ask around, find out who was looking after her. Check if she had a good home now that Petra wasn't around to care for her any more.

As I carried the three hot dogs oozing with ketchup and mustard back to my campsite, I could see both Dana and Molly waving their approval of my tasty lunchtime treat. They'd set up camp next to me with their folding tables, folding canvas chairs, water bottles, and tote-bags overflowing with essentials. Like chocolate bars, king-sized bags of chips, dog treats, grooming gear and a thermos of hot milky coffee. Penelope, too big for a playpen snoozed inside her large comfortable crate, while Molly's exuberant fox terrier, Busta, couldn't be trusted in an open playpen, so he was also crated between classes. Without even testing the theory, we'd all decided that if Busta was consigned to a doggy-playpen, we'd spend the entire show chasing him around the grounds. A playpen had yet to be invented that could keep Busta confined.

Penelope and Chloe weren't scheduled to compete in the Best Hound in Group class until later in the afternoon. So now it was time to kick back and relax. Coffee in one hand and hot dog in the other, we slouched in our chairs, coat collars pulled up around our ears, to protect us against the chill of the diligent South wind.

"Okay," said Dana stretching out her long legs. "Have either of you heard anything new on the show grapevine about Petra and Oliver's murders?"

"Not a thing," said Molly. "All seems like regurgitated news now."

"Actually, I have," I said, sipping on my coffee. "The Honorable Lady Felicity Taylor and Mr. Oliver T. Hutchins were once lovers."

That got their attention. I grinned as Dana almost dislocated her neck spinning around. "Lovers?" she repeated, mouth agape.

"At one stage they were engaged to be married. Don't know what went down, but it all ended badly. The theory around the show is that Felicity was keen to get back together with Oliver so she must have been murderous when she discovered he'd slept with Petra. And then, to add fuel to the fire, he put Petra's pug over her champion cocker spaniel for Best in Show." I lifted one eyebrow to get my point home. "Definitely a suspect, don't you think?"

"Definitely," echoed Dana. "She could have killed Petra, thinking if Petra was out the way she'd have a better chance with Oliver, but then when she went to his hotel room to tell him she still loved him, Oliver brushed her off. Laughed at her. Told her she was last week's news. Whatever. So, in a fit of pique, she killed him too."

Molly frowned and shook her head. "But if Lady Felicity went to the hotel room to make up with Oliver, tell him she loved him, why would she take a gun with her?"

"Hmm…you're right. If you're getting all dressed up for a lover's rendezvous, the last thing you'd slip in your favorite sparkly purse is a gun." I bent to fish a bag of chicken-flavored potato chips from my bag, tore the top off and offered the bag around. "Maybe we can scratch out Lady Felicity, but I did find something of importance while talking to Chi."

Dana's eyes lit up. "You did? Okay, spill the beans."

"Chi and Stephen were being blackmailed, first by Petra and then by Oliver."

"What for?"

"For feeding weed cookies to their dogs."

"You're joking."

"Wish I was. 'Cos now they seem to think *I'm* going to blackmail them too."

Molly's eyes widened as she leaned closer, eager to join in the speculation. "Petra must have found the marijuana cookies when she was at their kennels."

I nodded. "And *then* she was murdered…."

There was contemplative silence for all of twenty seconds before Dana tipped her head to one side. I could almost hear her brain cranking over as she tried to work through this new information. "Maybe Petra passed the info onto Oliver. Probably boasted about it to him while lying in bed together after sex." She blew out a sigh. "And after Petra was murdered, Oliver thought he could cash in too?"

"And then *he* was murdered…"

I had a sudden thought that sent my heart pummeling on my chest demanding to break out so it could run away and hide. "Oh, my God."

"You okay, Abi?" Molly leaned over and placed a comforting hand on my shoulder. "You've gone as white as those Samoyed dogs parading in ring three."

"I've just had a terrifying thought," My voice became more and more gravelly as it struggled to push through and around the lump in my throat. "If the two flamboyant poodle breeders murdered Petra and Oliver to stop them from destroying their reputation..."

Two pair of anxious eyes zeroed in on me.

"Now that *I* know about the illegal cookies, are they going to do away with me too?"

18

Five hours later, dressed in skinny jeans, long brown suede boots and a peach-colored turtleneck sweater under a three-quarter black coat, I perched on an unforgivingly hard wooden bench inside a rustic high-roofed pavilion that boasted of at least one hundred years' service. Adrenalin running on overdrive, my eyes were glued to the middle of the turfed arena. Where an athletic chestnut horse, ridden by a man in a red hunting coat, was currently leaping over a complicated course of colored obstacles, each higher than himself.

The only sounds from inside the pavilion were the *oohs* and *aahs* as the horse landed safely after each jump.

With a sausage and onion sandwich in one hand and a plastic cup half-full of coffee that tasted like burnt water in the other, I let out a gasp as the powerful horse soared over a blue and white oxer, the space between the poles wide enough to drive a bus through. Then the rider skillfully sat the horse back on his haunches in readiness for the following jump, a solitary rail with no ground line.

This was more exciting than watching my favorite X-Men movie. And funnily enough, I was enjoying myself more in the fresh air, numb bum camped on a hard bench and watching brave horses and riders worthy of an Olympic competition, than if I'd been surrounded by soft classical music, a high-priced menu and subtle table settings.

Some might say it was an unusual first date, but hey, I was snuggled up next to Nathan Forrester, my very own PI. My very own Mr. Nice Guy, who'd picked me up from home promptly at seven, nodded approvingly at my warm attire, and then whisked me off to the Adelaide Showgrounds to be entertained by a night of world-class showjumping, under lights. Eat your hearts out all you ladies out there on first dates dressed in tight clothes and uncomfortable high heels trying to make conversation while eating dinner at a restaurant.

Nathan, his body close to mine, grinned at my enthusiasm as I waved my half-eaten sandwich in the air and encouraged the big elegant chestnut, ridden by Nathan's childhood buddy, Mike, over the last mountainous obstacle on the course.

"And a clear round to Michael Steghorn, riding *Westwood Way Anker* with a time of 35.016 seconds," the commentator boomed. "This puts them in the lead with only three competitors left to go in the jump-off. Steghorn's jumping machine, *Westwood Way Anker* has won five World Cup events this year. Three in Victoria, two in New South Wales and if they win tonight's event, they'll be representing Australia at the World Cup final in Germany later this year."

"How long's your friend been involved with horses?" I asked around a mouthful of sausage.

Nathan's laugh was that same rich chocolatey sound that attracted me to him in his office. "Ever since primary school days and then we ended up at the same University. He used to invite me around to his house and we'd go off on the ponies for hours."

"So, you ride too. That's something else I've learned about you tonight."

He grinned. "And it won't be the last."

Time to change the subject. "Um…so, why did he go to university when all he wanted to do was ride horses?"

"His father insisted. Made him study for his business degree before helping him set up a riding academy. Mike's been training and competing full time since the day after he graduated."

I could tell just how proud Nathan was of his friend. His eyes lit up after he completed his round and ten minutes later, his grip on my hand tightened as we waited for the final rider to navigate the course. One jump down. Which meant Michael Steghorn and his big handsome chestnut warmblood, *Westward Way Anker*, aka Brutus, were off to Germany to represent Australia.

As the stand began to clear of spectators, Nathan stood up. "Want to visit the stables before we go home? I need to prick Mike's balloon, otherwise he'll be so damn cocky I won't be able to keep him in his place."

He reached out a hand for me.

Okay, I mightn't be a gym-tragic or a dedicated early morning jogger, but I *could* stand up without assistance. However, unable to resist Nathan's gentlemanly offer, I slipped my hand into his. Instead of pulling me up, his hand hugged mine, warm and intimate, like the glint in his eyes. Immediately my throat went dry, my heart did a three-point cartwheel and certain bits below the belt began to quiver. Whoa! If Nathan Forrester could make me feel like this with a squeeze of his hand, what the heck could he do to me if his hand strayed to other parts of my body?

"Hey, no need to prick any balloons." My laugh sounded more like a frog's croak as I stood up, breaking the spell. "The guy's just won a trip to Germany to show the world what the best riders in Australia can do."

"You don't know Mike like I do," he said, taking my hand again. "He'll be so cheeky and cocky he'll be full of it. Need an air rifle or a dart gun to bring him down to earth again."

Holding hands, we strolled across the Showgrounds toward the stable block. As we approached, the smell of fresh hay drifted on the cold night air. That distinct aroma that horse lovers the world over breathe in, hold, and smile, eyes closed, as they exhale. The four-beat clump of metal shoes striking the cement as horses were led into the hose-down bays or back to their warm stables. The rattling of oats in buckets, the swishing of brooms as groom and riders cleared shavings from the front of their allotted stable.

The world of professional showjumping and the world of pony club kids who only dream of becoming showjumping stars are virtually the same. Only the ages and the achievements differ.

We found Michael Steghorn in one of the wash-bays hosing down his horse, Brutus. The powerful chestnut appeared taller and more commanding at close range and his owner's grin was so wide it almost slid off his face. "Hey, Spyglass," he yelled when he spotted Nathan. "You made it!"

Guys and their nicknames. I guessed Spyglass originated from Nathan's unusual profession.

"Wouldn't miss it, mate. Congratulations." Nathan's eyes twinkled as he shook his head, face mock serious. "However, I did detect a slight error on your part turning into the RM Williams jump after the treble. Lucky you had a good horse under you or the jump would have been left in splinters."

Michael swished the hose and almost caught Nathan with a squirt of water. "You mean like at the Pony Club championships back in the day when you ended up flat on your back in the middle of the Road Closed jump? And when your pony took off out of the ring and almost mowed down one of the gate stewards?"

"Yeah, exactly." Nathan laughed. "I was 10 years old, the pony you lent me to ride that day was as crazy as a loon and I'd been in bed with the flu all week. But you're never going to let me live it down, are you?"

"Nope." Mike shook his head, eyes brimming with mischief.

After dodging another poorly aimed squirt, Nathan draped an arm around my shoulders, pulling me up against his hard body. "Hey, Mike, I'd like you to meet a very special friend of mine, Abigail Truelove."

"Hi, Michael," I said giving him no time to come up with a witty comment about my surname and eyeing off the beautiful chestnut horse pawing the ground in the hose-bay. "Love your horse. He's amazing. Had him long?"

"Seven years. Bought Brutus as a just-broken-in gangly three-year-old. Knew there was something special about him the day I arrived at the farm and saw him leap over a five-foot fence from a standstill to escape from a yard into a paddock where he could see other horses getting fed." I watched as Michael stroked the big strong chestnut's neck and played with the long shiny forelock that fell in waves between the horse's ears. Pride and love shone from his eyes. "This guy and I have been through a lot together to get to that win today." He closed his fist and pumped the air. "And now we're off to Germany for the World Cup finals. Yahoo!"

While Mike and Nathan performed a customized hi-five sequence known only to them, I took in the activity around us. It was loud. It was chaotic. And yet it was organized. Horses, although beautiful and talented and adored by their owners, are also big, dangerous and highly strung and horse people tend to always think of their animal first. So, although there was a sea of high spirits lapping around us, it was controlled.

A group of well-wishers had started to descend on Michael, so, feeling a little like an outsider, I took a few steps back away from the hose-bay.

And that's when I saw him…

Luke.

Well, it looked like Luke. Red, yellow and blue-striped Crows footy scarf around his neck and bundled up in a bottle-green puffer coat like the one I bought him for his last birthday. He darted in between several jodhpur-clad individuals gathered around a big grey horse being led up and down by a girl in khaki overalls at the end of the stable block. All studying the horse's gait.

But what would Luke be doing at a horse show? The only horses he was ever interested in were those he watched on TV. The ones he screamed abuse at when they weren't first past the post.

I craned my neck to get a better view but the Luke-lookalike had disappeared in the crowd. Maybe I was mistaken. After all, those bottle-green puffer coats were popular this winter and going for a bargain price at Big W, Target and K-Mart stores. And as for the Crow's scarf…half South Australia's population followed the football team.

Frowning, I turned back to listen to Nathan as he took my hand and led me away from the crush of enthusiastic well-wishers jostling around the horses. "Let's get out of here, Abi. The journos have arrived and Mike's about to be inundated with photographers and other media types."

"Okay." I pushed the thought of Luke out of my mind and squeezed Nathan's hand. Even if Luke was here, what did that have to do with me? His life was his own now.

"I know a little eatery in the middle of town that specializes in delicious desserts. Can I interest you in joining me?"

"Delicious desserts?" I grinned my agreement at his thinking. "Hey, does a spider have eight legs?"

Nathan's hand still clasped in mine, we walked across the road and entered the almost empty car park. Most spectators had already left. Gone home to snuggle up on the lounge with TV and nibbles or to their local pub to socialize with friends. The showjumping wannabees back to their stables to talk to their horses and dream of their future.

Michael Steghorn now their idol.

The gravel crunched underfoot as we made our way to Nathan's car. "So far I've only learned one more thing about you tonight," I told him with a dig to his ribs. "That you were a crap rider as a kid."

He feigned indignation. "Hey, only because Mike made me ride the ponies he was too scared to get on himself. If they didn't buck me off, then he'd try them out. Which makes *me* a better rider than him."

"Hmm…maybe you should have gone in for stunt riding instead of becoming a private investigator."

A large dark-colored car, the only vehicle left in the next lane over, started its engine with a rumbling growl, its headlights on low beam. Hardly enough light to navigate its way out of the dimly lit carpark.

"Actually, I can see myself as a stuntman," said Nathan, one arm around my shoulders as we walked. "You know, galloping a half-broke mustang down a steep mountain in The Man from Snowy River."

"Mmm…although I don't think the bush clothes would suit you. Dirty moleskins, scuffed boots and unwashed hair covered by an unflattering bush hat. Maybe you'd make a better James Bond stuntman. You might end up with two broken legs and a couple of cracked ribs but at least you'd be dressed in *Dolce and Gabbana*."

He laughed. "Okay, okay, stunt riding is not my forte."

"Well, what is? I still have to learn four more things about you before saying goodnight."

The dark colored car continued to squat there, in its parking bay in the next lane, motor rumbling, lights still on low beam. Someone was in no hurry to get home. And then with a jerk, it reversed, straightened up, nose pointed toward the exit, but going nowhere.

"What would you like to know?" We were three cars away from Nathan's silver Lexus. He came to a stop and turned to face me. "And then, Abigail Truelove, I think it's only fair that you tell me five things about you. Okay?"

Five things about me? Holy chickenfeed. I gave a reluctant nod. What was I going to reveal? That I was a compulsive chocaholic? Had a secret love affair with crispy crème donuts? Hated wearing tight knickers that crept into unmentionable cracks. And that I owned a never-ending supply of oversized sloppy tees that I wore to bed with not a stitch underneath?

Maybe this wasn't such a good idea after all.

I imagine Nathan Forrester, the well credentialed PI, would only be interested in a woman with good taste in clothes and habits, a full social life and the appetite of a gnat. In other words – the opposite of me.

"Okay, here goes," His eyes sparkled in the half-light as he lifted one hand to tuck a lock of hair behind my ears. I liked the feel of his warm fingers as they grazed my cheek. "Number one – I'm a pizza junkie."

"You are?" I grinned. Maybe this soul-baring wouldn't be so bad after all. "Hey, I could eat pizza every night of the week, as long as it was followed up by Krispy Krème donuts or a tub of Ben & Jerry's ice cream."

"Number two – I'm never happier than when I can ditch my office clothes and drag on an old pair of jeans and a tee shirt and go digging in the garden or messing around with the dogs at my parents' house."

My grin spread further. "Okay, and here's another one for me. When I was little, I wanted to be a ballerina. Even now, when no-one's around, I dance in the kitchen, pretend I'm the dying swan in Swan Lake, or practice pliés in front of the mirror."

We'd reached Nathan's car and instead of clicking the remote to open the doors, he leaned against the bonnet and folded his arms. His lips twitched and even in the half-light I could see the mischief in his eyes. "Righto. Let's have a preview. I want to see you dance."

"No. Not here."

"Go on, show me a few spins."

"Pirouettes?"

Making himself comfortable against the front of the car, he nodded. "Yeah. Those too."

This was so embarrassing. The reason I didn't become a ballerina was because I was more elephant than dainty deer when it came to dancing. Something I found out very early on when my mum had given in and taken me for lessons. But just because I was a lead-footed dancer didn't stop me from dancing in the privacy of my own home.

In the middle of a carpark? Not so much.

I stood there, hands to my sides, debating, and finally let out a laugh. "Okay, *Spyglass*," I said borrowing from the nickname his friend had used. "As it turned out, I'm a lousy ballerina. However, that doesn't mean I can't do half a dozen pirouettes to satisfy your warped sense of humor. Okay? Just stand well clear because I'm likely to get giddy, lose control and knock you over."

"This I have to see," said the man twinkling at me from a prime view in front of his car.

"I haven't done this for a while, so if I fall over and embarrass myself, I won't be happy." I pointed my toe to the side, lifted my arms ready to perform the first of my set of six pirouettes and sent him one last eye lift. "Don't say I didn't warn you."

The car came out of nowhere.

The snarl of an over-engaged engine behind me didn't fully register until I felt Nathan's arms lift me off the ground, spiraling me into the air as the car grazed my right hip and raced on, tires screaming.

After what felt like two minutes in the air but was probably less than two heart-beats, I slammed into the ground so hard I swear my kidneys almost fell out of my ears.

Then watched, dazed, as the dark car, arrogant in its victory, spewed gravel in its wake before roaring out of the car park.

*****

My right hip burned. I moved my leg. No unbearable pain. No break. Just a badly bruised hip. Thank you, God. A sharp rock dug into the middle of my back but I couldn't have stood up right then if a herd of crazed zombies were lumbering toward me.

The driver of that car had deliberately tried to run me down. Why?

"Abi, Abi, are you hurt?"

I blinked. Tried to focus. Nathan's anxious face peered down at me. His fingers gently smoothed my hair from my eyes. "You're scaring me, Abi. Say something."

I licked my dry lips, took a shaky breath. "You certainly know how to give a girl an exciting first date. Do you throw all your girlfriends around like that?"

His laugh was high-pitched, and I could see the worry ooze out, quickly replaced by action. He tugged his phone from his pocket and within seconds he'd phoned the police and propped me up against the side of the nearest car.

"Who have you pissed off lately?"

I shook my head which didn't help my raging headache. Merely strengthened its ferocity. "Dunno. Although there was that snarky lady who came into *Pampered Pooch* a few days ago and went all psycho when I asked her to clean up her dog's wee. There's a mop and a bucket of warm soapy water underneath a sign in the shop that says, 'Your dog – your mess'." I knew I was babbling. Could stop. Tried to smile to offset Nathan's concern, but the muscles around my mouth refused to co-operate. Must have looked like rigor mortis had set in.

"Who knows you've been investigating Petra and Oliver's murders?"

I thought of all the questions I'd been asking at the dog show, the way we'd infiltrated suspects' properties, made accusations against those who'd bought a *Chanel* lead from my shop, and my stomach did a sickening backflip and landed with a squeamish thud. Goosebumps sprung up, prickling and threatening to take over my entire body. Stephen? Chi? Luke? Wild Bill? Geez, any one of those could have been behind the wheel of that car.

And their mission – close the big mouth – splatter her across the carpark – make sure she can't ask any more questions.

"Abi, who have you been investigating?"

My voice came out like it had been dragged across sharp gravel. "Everyone who bought *Chanel* leads from the *Pampered Pooch*."

"Why didn't you leave it to the police?"

"Nathan, you know why. The police closed the case after Oliver's confession."

He let out a sigh. "I know, I know. It's just that I don't want you hurt." His fingers traced lightly over the bump on my head from where I'd hit the ground when he threw me out of harm's way. Nathan Forrester had saved my life. He cleared his throat. "Is there anyone specific who'd want you dead?"

"Well, I thought I saw Luke hanging around the horse-stables at the showgrounds." My voice had to push through a sudden tightness in my throat. Surely Luke, my ex-boyfriend wouldn't try to run me down. That didn't make sense. Unless he'd killed Petra and Oliver and wanted me out of the way too.

"What the hell was *he* doing there?"

"Don't know. And I don't know if it really *was* him. I-I just saw a man who looked like Luke darting through the crowd."

I could hear the thud of footsteps approaching us at a fast clip and gripped Nathan's hand tighter.

"Abi? Abi? Are you okay?" I looked up to see Luke himself, eyes wide, hair standing on end, running toward me. He was with a woman in her early twenties. Black boots, black dress, black coat, black eye-makeup and as uncoordinated as a two-day old filly.

"Luke?" I blinked up at him. Unless he'd ditched the car, grown a set of wings and flown back to the scene of the crime, it wasn't Luke who'd been driving the lethal weapon.

"I saw that car knock you over. It was deliberate. He lined you up and went straight for you. Oh, my, God, I thought he'd killed you."

Nathan turned to Luke. "Did you get the car's registration number?"

Luke did a double-take. He frowned at Nathan. "Hey, you're that cop guy from the other night."

"Yes, yes, I'm that cop-guy. Now, did you get the car's registration?"

Luke shook his head. "Nah. Happened too quickly. Too worried about Abi."

Nathan didn't answer but his expression said, *Idiot! Should have been the first thing you did.*

This wasn't the time for an all-out-testosterone-fueled war, so, with the help of both Nathan and Luke, I tested out my legs by pushing up off the ground. Sore hip, but otherwise okay. Just shaky. Nothing that a good hot bath wouldn't fix. A bath with a touch of rosemary, Epsom salts and maybe a squirt of that old faithful liniment, Penetrine. And then a night snuggled up in bed with Chloe, catching up on sleep. Although I had my doubts there. More like horrific nightmares reliving the rushing sound of that car and the painful shock as it ploughed into me.

"What are you doing here at the showjumping?" I asked Luke, still not sure if his concern was real. "You're not stalking me, are you?"

"Stalking you? No, no. Emily's into horses and I'm here with her. You've got it all wrong, Abi."

"Have I? What about the restraining order brought against you by your previous girlfriend?"

Luke ran a stiff hand though his hair. "Since our break-up, I've been to three counseling sessions. Even joined an anger management group." He turned to the Goth standing shyly beside him. "That's where I met Emily who'd recently come out of a bad relationship with a guy who used his fists instead of words. Made me realize how, if I want a lasting and loving relationship in the future, I need to change." With an arm around her shoulders, he snuggled the woman closer. "And Emily's helping me. Came to speak about her ordeal at the meeting and we just clicked the moment our eyes met."

A police car, siren wailing, swerved into the carpark and screeched to a halt beside us. I let out a sigh of relief. Prematurely, as it turned out, as my nemesis, DI Lightfoot stepped out and the rapidity and repetitiveness of the questions that followed quickly had my already aching head craving aspirins, whisky and a nice lay-down.

If only…

At last, Lightfoot and his partner, a curry-faced female constable who didn't attempt to soothe me with a 'there, there, everything will be alright, we'll catch the bad guy' platitude, like they do on TV, finally climbed back into the police car and prepared to leave.

Engine running, the DI poked his head out the open window. "By the way, Ms. Truelove, can you let your friend from *The Pussycat Parlor* know she left one of her silver high-heeled shoes behind when we sprung her in the early hours of Tuesday morning? My front-desk sergeant did try to contact her but she's not answering her phone. Tell her she can pick it up any time. It's at the front desk."

"Tuesday morning?" I frowned. "I thought you didn't discharge Sharon until Wednesday morning."

"Had nothing to hold her on. When we took her in after you discovered the deceased in the alley way, we questioned her further and then let her go." He slipped the gears into drive, revved the engine. "Anyway, if you see her, tell her to call in when she's passing that way again."

My brain, already a little off-center due to my head bouncing off the hard ground, took another convoluted spin. What was the DI saying? That Sharon hadn't been held in a cell until Wednesday morning like she'd led me to believe. She'd been released early on the same morning she was taken in for further questioning. Why didn't she pick up her dog after leaving the police station? Why lie to me?

And then another thought like a big black wrecking-ball smashed into my already overloaded brain cells…

Pussy Willow, aka Sharon Bottomley, had strong motivation for murdering Petra, and now no alibi for when the show-judge was killed.

19

Late Sunday morning, I woke to find Chloe licking my face asking to be let out, a very *ouchy* bump on my head and a bruise the size and shape of a large rat on my right hip. And speaking of rats, I'd decided to pay Sharon Bottomley a visit at *The Pussycat Parlor*. I'd been told the dancers met every Sunday around 11am to work on new routines. A perfect time to interrogate her.

Slipping into a dressing gown which had mysteriously mislaid its belt, I shuffled from the bedroom into the kitchen. Poor Chloe hopped along beside me, stumpy little legs crossed, an anxious bug-eyed expression on her face. The moment I opened the back door to the garden she shot through the opening like a racing greyhound exploding from the chutes and as soon as her paws hit the lawn, she lowered her back end to the ground and moaned in ecstasy.

After paying attention to my own urgent toileting needs, I let Chloe back into the house and made us a late breakfast. Scrambled eggs on toast for me and a bowl of Doggy-doo dry for Chloe. It was a race to see who cleaned their plate first, but as usual, Chloe won. Her tongue more active than mine. She cocked her head to one side and grinned up at me, and I swear the little wiener dog was laughing. She knew what a sucker I was for her puppy-dog eyes. Knew she'd end up with a sliver of my toast and a blob of scrambled egg for 'afters'.

The night before, after I'd refused to go to the hospital to be checked out, Nathan drove me home, made sure I knew what day it was and how many fingers he was holding up. He offered to spend the night on the couch and wasn't at all put out when I told him to stop acting like a Dutch Uncle and go home. And then, he'd shot my Dutch Uncle analogy down in sizzling hot flames with a goodnight kiss that virtually blew the socks right off my feet.

Still feeling a little woozy, I headed for the shower and a change of clothes. Skinny jeans, Cuban-heeled boots, and the warmest sweater in my bottom drawer. Emerald green with a turtle-neck. And because the wind was icy cold outside, a light jacket.

If I didn't get a move on, I'd miss out on catching up with Sharon. And I needed answers to my questions. Number one on the list – why did she lie about when she'd been let out of jail?

The Pussycat Parlor appeared more run down and far-less exciting by daylight. No bright colored lights flickering outside. No loud raucous music blaring through the front door. And no drunk patrons staggering to waiting taxis.

Just the quiet of a normal Sunday morning in suburbia.

I found a parking spot in front of the nightclub, lined up with the arch over the entrance and switched the engine off. After making sure my extra-strong lethal can of hair-spray was still buried inside my tote-bag – you never know when you might need a weapon – I clicked the remote to secure the car and marched up to the front door. Bolted shut. Wouldn't you know it? I gave the door a shake, knocked, plastered my nose against the glass and peered inside, but no one materialized out of the gloom to let me in.

Damn.

Seemed like if I wanted to get inside the nightclub to find Sharon, I'd need to locate a staff entrance. There was no way I was going around to the back alley and use the staff entrance there. Even at 11.30 on a Sunday morning, when the rats had retreated to their home under the dumpster, even with a weak sun trying to break through the clouds overhead, there was no way I could walk down that alley again without seeing Petra's poor dead twisted body staring back up at me from the cold tarmac.

The sound of faint music coming from behind a door closer to the corner of the building had me heading in that direction. Music meant dancers. And dancers meant *Pussy Willow* aka Sharon, aka the owner of the intrepid Mimi, might be practicing her strip-tease routine on the other side of that wall.

I slid the door open just far enough to poke my head around the corner. Didn't want to barge in on a completed strip-tease act and incinerate the corneas in my eyes.

Eight women of various sizes and ages, dressed in typical working outfits of laddered tights and skimpy boob-tubes, hair either drooping after their previous night's work or dragged back into a pony tail, were going through a dance-routine. Satisfied, I slipped all the way into the room but kept to the shadows so as not to distract them from their practice.

A whale of a guy, half-smoked cigarette protruding from the corner of his bloated lips, squatted on a padded stool at the piano. His fat sausage fingers thumped away at the keys. His elephantine buttocks hung over both sides of the stool like sides of meat on a rack. Next to him posed a thin weasel guy, sharp-nosed, pockmarked face and sporting tight black trousers and a gaudy top, his lascivious eyes running up and down the women's bodies like he owned every inch of them.

One dancer, barely old enough to have finished high school, stopped in the middle of the routine to hop up and down and rub her left calf. Obviously cramp. But Weasel Guy screamed at her, told her if she couldn't keep up with the others to go look for a job at McDonald's. When the music stopped, he spat on the floor, glared at the now sniffing dancer with the cramp and let out a low growl. "For God sake, Chrissie, get out of my sight. Go and get Barry to give you a rub down or *something*. I don't want to see your face again until he's given you a do-over."

As the offending dancer limped through a doorway leading to the rear of the nightclub Weasel-guy turned on the others. "What is it with you lazy broads?" he yelled, and I was surprised the volume didn't cause a crack in the nearest window. "My 80-year-old grandma has better moves than you lot. I wanna see that again. And this time give me more oomph, more sex, more tits and arse. Your job is to make the punters horny, not take you home to mother." He grabbed what looked like a handkerchief sized scrap of material from the top of the piano and held it up for them to see. "For our new number we're going *Tropical Tangerine*. Okay? Think erotic tangerine. Tangerine sparkles. Tangerine feathers. And see-through bras with tangerine sequins. Your costumes will be ready for fitting this time on Tuesday."

"Not *orange*, Marty," wailed *Pussy Willow* her face screwed up like she could smell maggoty fish. "You know what I think of *orange!* It's toxic. Hideous. Brings me nothing but bad luck. Last time you forced orange on me, I didn't get one tip all week. I'm telling you, Marty. Orange doesn't suit me!"

Orange doesn't suit me?

The exact words used in Oliver T Hutchins's phony confession?

Something cold and slimy tiptoed up my spine.

Coincidence?

Or was *Pussy Willow* our murderer?

*****

With one hand on the door ready to ease it open, slither through, and make a discreet getaway, I glanced over my shoulder and froze. Sharon was watching me. Staring at me. At first her face registered confusion and then, judging by the tightening of her lips, the stark chill in her eyes and the way her body puffed up like a snake ready to strike, I figured she knew. Knew I'd put two and two together and come up with her as the author of Oliver's phony 'confession.'

I didn't wait to find out what she was going to do about it. My hand trembled as I nudged the door open and stumbled through onto the street. As my feet slapped the pavement, I tried to run but my legs had the muscle-power of cooked spaghetti and my breath hit the air in noisy pants. This woman was a killer. She'd already done away with two people and because I'd figured this out – I'd likely be next in the queue.

As I forced my shaky legs in the direction of the van it was like I was slogging through deep viscous mud. Fifty meters became a marathon. Finding my keys to click the car doors open became a life or death situation.

Before throwing first my bag and then myself behind the wheel, I checked to see if Sharon had followed me.

The street was empty.

Okay, I'd drive like the clappers to my house, send an SOS to Dana and Molly and when they arrived, we'd barricade the front door with as much furniture as we could drag across. Then, once we were safe, brainstorm how to convince the police to charge Sharon for Petra and Oliver's murder with no evidence other than the color *'orange didn't suit her'* and she'd lied to me about where she was at the time Oliver was murdered.

Piece of cake? *Not.*

Traffic along Port Road proved to be bumper to bumper. Argh…Seemed like every 500 meters workmen dressed in lime-colored *hi-viz* vests and armed with a shovel or an iPad were turning cars into creeping caterpillars and drivers into frustrated zombies. I'd have been quicker going the long way. At one 'road works in progress' sign, a bald guy using a shovel as a prop while holding up a red stop sign seemed to forget he was in charge of traffic and went into a dream state.

While waiting for Bald Guy to wake up and wave the traffic on, I rummaged in my bag, snaffled my phone and by the time the red stop sign was replaced with green, I'd sent emergency texts off to Dana and Molly.

I know who killed Petra and Oliver. We are all in danger. Drop everything and meet me at my place. ASAP.

Glancing at the time on the dash, I dropped the phone in my pocket. I'd been driving for twenty minutes over a distance which normally took ten.

Eeek!

One eye on the rear vision mirror as I drove, I checked to see if I was being followed. Duh! An entire cavalcade of cars filled my rear mirror.

Any one of them could have Sharon parked behind the wheel, an axe, a gun, and a hypodermic syringe vying for attention on the seat beside her. I thought back to the morning she'd come to pick up Mimi. What car was she driving? I hadn't really paid much attention at the time as I was running late for work and had a visit to the police station to fit in as well. I remembered it was yellow. And small. Maybe a Kia or a Yaris? Once again, I squinted into the rear-view mirror and then the side mirror. Only yellow car I could see in the all-encompassing traffic was a family-sized SUV. Definitely not Sharon.

Maybe I was being paranoid. Maybe Sharon hadn't realized that I'd figured out she was the author of Oliver's email confession. Yeah, and maybe the world was flat. I'd seen comprehension harden her eyes. Retaliation in the set of her jaw. She knew. And she was going to do something about it.

There were no cars parked out the front of my house when I turned into the driveway. Which meant neither Dana nor Molly had arrived yet. But also, no Sharon.

I switched off the engine, grabbed my bag and scrambled out of the car. The sooner I was inside the safety of my house with the doors and windows locked, the police on speed-dial and my two friends beside me, the better.

I checked my phone. No answer to my texts. Oh God, maybe Molly had switched her phone off and was so absorbed with fitting Sebastian's Tab A into Rebecca's Slot B that she hadn't received my warning. And Dana? How could she drop everything as I'd stipulated in my text? Where do you find a babysitter at a minute's notice? With a sigh, I dropped the phone back into my coat pocket and straightened my shoulders.

It looked like I was on my own.

And then the oddity registered in my zapped-out brain. When I left to go to the *Pussycat Parlor* this morning, I'd left the roller-door on the carport up. Now it was down. Not all the way. Just enough that if I bent down and looked underneath, I could see a small yellow car.

A yellow car with the registration number SEX 835.

20

Shards of ice slammed up against my heart causing it to judder like an out-of-control bulldozer. My feet seemed to sink into the ground as though I'd stepped in quicksand. I couldn't move. And yet I had to. I had to get back in my car and drive away as fast as I could. Drive to the nearest police station and if they wouldn't come and take Sharon away, I'd smash one of their windows, so they'd arrest me and lock me in the safety of a cell.

I tried to lift my feet, but I was still knee-deep in quicksand, the messages from my brain to my legs distorted by static. What about Dana and Molly? I had to send them a text telling them not to come near my house. Warn them that the big bad wolf was already in residence.

But first I had to get the hell out of there. With the fear that Molly or Dana could pull up any minute, I forced my feet to move in the direction of my car. My mind lasered in on the action of one foot after the other.

"Going somewhere, Abi?"

I spun around.

It was Sharon. "Going somewhere and not taking your dog with you? That makes you a bad dog mother and there's nothing worse than a bad dog mother."

Still dressed in tights and hot pink boob top with a long black coat thrown over the top, she stood by the front door of my house. A crazed smirk twitching at the corners of her lips. And my wide-eyed dachshund squirming in her arms.

Time stood still and the world fell away as I stared at the barrel of a gun, only centimeters from my darling Chloe's head.

"Oh God, nooo! Please, Sharon. Don't hurt Chloe. This is between you and me – not Chloe." My voice cracked as I moved away from the car, eyes glued to the dog in her arms. Hearing the panic in my voice, Chloe whined and squirmed even harder. She wanted to get down and come to me. I had to do something. If Chloe didn't stop wriggling the gun might accidentally go off.

"Up to you," Sharon said and shook her head. "But if you don't want your dog's brains splattered over your doorstep, walk inside, very slowly. I'll be right behind you."

If I went through that doorway, I'd be dead. But what else could I do? I checked up and down the street. Only person in sight was old Mr. Taylor three doors down and with cataracts in both eyes and sandwich thick glasses, he could barely see three inches in front of his nose. I glanced across at the house next door. No one. Where were your neighbors when you needed them? In your face gossiping when you were late for work but not even twitching a curtain at the window when your life was in danger.

"Hurry up. My left arm's aching from holding this long lump of sausage you call a dog and my right arm's aching from stopping the gun from going off. Get yourself inside or I won't be able to keep the two apart."

Unable to think of a way out, I moved toward the doorway. If only Nathan would rock up in his silver car, flash his fake police badge again and save the day.

Yeah, that only happened in romance novels.

"Ditch your bag on the doorstep before you go inside. We don't want phones, scissors or whatever else you have stashed in that tote to cause any problems between us, now do we?"

Phone?

Of course. My phone was in my jacket pocket…not my bag.

If I could inadvertently slip my hand into my pocket and touch redial, I might be able to connect with whoever I'd spoken to last. If they answered they'd hear what was going on. Maybe ring the police.

Okay, a long shot, but a long shot was better than a bullet to the gut.

"But Sharon, I can't do that. It's a Saint Laurent bag." Okay, a knock-off Saint Laurent but she didn't need to know that. I held my bag up in front of me with one hand to show her, while unobtrusively feeling around in my pocket with the other. "If I leave my bag out here, someone might steal it."

She shook her head in mock sympathy. "Don't worry, Abi, where you're going, you'll have no use for a bag. Saint Laurent or a Target special."

"You won't get away with this Sharon. I've already informed several people you killed Petra and Oliver. If I'm found dead here in my house, you're the first person the police will arrest. You'll spend the rest of your life in the color you hate. Orange."

Big words. Big bluff. No need to tell her it was only Molly and Dana I'd informed, via text, and I hadn't even given them a name.

She didn't answer, merely tightened her grip on Chloe and waved me inside with a flick of the gun. With nothing left in my arsenal, I dropped my tote on the front verandah and edged through the doorway. The latch clicked on the door as it closed behind me sending gnarly hobgoblins to play leapfrog in my stomach. Then, as I headed for the lounge room, a sharp pain in my right ankle announced the arrival of Sharon's totally ungrateful and Queen of Mean, Pomeranian, Mimi. When was this nightmare going to end? I shook my leg and the dog latched on harder. "Ouch!" Her vampire teeth felt like they'd been sharpened to points with a file, especially for my benefit.

"Now, fasten these handcuffs around your wrists and sit in that chair while I figure out how to make your death look like an accident." Sharon dropped Chloe onto the floor and pulled a set of handcuffs out of her pocket. Where did she get handcuffs? Sexual fantasies carried out with clients at the *Pussycat Parlor?* Or stolen from the police station when the duty sergeant wasn't looking?

Chloe yelped as she hit the polished floorboards. Soft brown eyes bewildered, confused, hurt, she scrambled to her feet and scuttled across the room to me, tail buried between her legs. My fists clenched at my side, nails biting into the skin while something red-hot and primal stabbed at my heart, quickly building into a well-fueled bonfire. Ignoring the handcuffs at my feet, I swooped Chloe up and cuddled her to my chest. Her cold nose grazed my cheek and her body trembled as she snuggled deeper into my shoulder. I glared at the cause of my dog's distress and the words, *'You'll pay!'* kept repeating over and over like a mantra in my head.

But raw emotion would only get us *both* killed.

I sucked in a deep breath. Dampened the blazing fire within. The only way to save Chloe's life was to reason with the woman in charge of the gun. Only then, would I be able to figure out a way to save mine. "Don't hurt Chloe, Sharon. Let me put her outside in the yard. She's not involved in any of this. You have Mimi. You're a dog lover too."

Mimi, dressed in a Swan Lake tutu and white satin bootees, had let go of my ankle and rushed across to check on Chloe when she'd hit the floor. Now she sat at my feet, gazing up at me. Was she asking to be picked up? Was she worried about Chloe?

Maybe there was hope for the psycho dog yet.

Sharon let out a frustrated sigh as she stomped across the room and threw the back door wide open. "No other person in my situation would do this. Why me? Why am *I* so nice?"

Yeah, so nice you murdered two people and was now planning on how to kill a third and make it look like an accident.

"Well, come on," she said glaring at me. "Toss that mutt of yours down on the floor. She can go outside with Mimi, keep her company until I've finished what I came here to do."

Cuddling Chloe to my chest, I walked toward the door. "If I put her down, she won't leave me. The only way she'll go outside is if I put her out there myself."

Sharon took a step away from the open doorway, trained the gun on me. I turned my back to her as I carried Chloe outside. Was she aiming at my heart? Head? Kidneys? Oh God, I didn't want the pain of a bullet smashing into any part of me. Not even my little pinky finger.

How the heck did I end up in this situation? I was a normal twenty-eight-year-old with all the usual characteristics of a woman my age. I scoffed ice cream and chocolate when I was stressed. I tried to pay my bills on time but sometimes a special pair of shoes got in the way. I enjoyed driving to the country or the beach in Spring and Summer. Yet here I was, my back exposed to a mad woman with a gun. A mad woman who'd already disposed of two lives as though they were crumpled-up, unwanted trash for the bin.

I could rush her, attempt to knock the gun out of her hand. I could head-butt her in the stomach. Or I could run. Take off and hope to get out of bullet range before she pulled the trigger.

Muscles tense, I turned around to face her, but one look at the murder in her eye and the way the gun was leveled, not at my pinky finger but at the middle of my heart told me this wasn't the time to act. I needed her distracted, at least looking the other way before I made a move. I kissed Chloe on the nose, ran a gentle hand over her ears, placed her on the ground and gave her a gentle push away from me.

Sharon waved the gun. "Now, back inside!"

No other option but to obey.

The moment I was inside, the door slammed shut behind me like the lid of a coffin closing before the screws were tightened and it was lowered into the ground.

I grabbed a breath. Decided I needed to keep her talking. "I guess you were the driver of that car that tried to run me down last night?"

Her answer was a chillingly flat smile. A smile that reminded me of a vampire, seconds before piercing your carotid artery and feeding on your blood.

"But yours is yellow, Sharon. Did you steal that dark colored car?"

Hey!" she growled. Flicked her long hair off her shoulders. "I'm no thief!" *No, just a murderer.* "I *borrowed* the car from Boris, the doorman at the Pussycat Parlor."

"Why? So *he'd* be charged if anyone reported the rego number?"

"Just fasten the handcuffs around your wrists, sit on the chair and shut up. My arm's getting tired of holding this gun, so I might just shoot you now and work out what to do with your body after."

"Forensics will know I've been killed here in my house," I said, my voice surprisingly matter-of-fact considering the situation. "Blood splatter."

"I'll clean up any blood before I take your body out into the country and dump it. Maybe I'll send you and your car over a cliff. That could work."

"Forensics have a special blue light they shine on surfaces to pick up blood splatter," I told her, my stomach slamming into my toes at the thought of me and my car hurtling over a cliff. "Doesn't matter how hard you scrub, how much cleaning fluid you use, the blood splatter patterns remain."

"If you're not sitting on that chair by the time I finish cocking this gun, you'll be splattered all over the room." She smirked, her mad eyes widening. "That'll give the forensic team plenty to play with, won't it?"

Okay. That didn't sound like a lot of fun. I picked the handcuffs up off the floor, sat down and fastened them around my wrists. The handcuffs might slow me down, but I still had my legs and my wits to work with.

By now I had no idea if the phone in my pocket was working or not. No idea if the person I'd spoken to last had even picked up. And with my brain drowning in icy water and so intent on devising a plan to stay alive, I couldn't even remember who I'd rung last.

But in case it was still working, I had to get a confession out of Sharon. Even if I ended up a dead body at the bottom of a cliff, my phone might still be intact and incriminate her. And best-case scenario, whoever was on the other end of the phone might have decided I wasn't playing a role in a stage play and contacted the police.

"Don't you think it was rather extreme to kill Petra because your friend committed suicide?" I had to keep her talking. "After all, Petra might have dumped the guy, but it was your friend's decision to kill himself, not hers."

Sharon's face twisted into a mask of ugly. "That *friend* was actually my brother. My baby brother who was already riddled with depression before Petra got her claws into him. She, that monster, tossed him over the edge and then laughed about it. Called him a babbling idiot. A moron not worthy of life." Sharon slammed one hand down on the table so hard the cup at the end shook, then toppled to the floor and smashed. "*She* was the one babbling when I slipped the leash around her neck. Babbling so much she wet herself when I pulled it tight. She couldn't believe it was happening. Tried to kick me but I soon put a stop to that with a fist in her tarted-up face. And when she eventually gave in and stopped struggling, I knew she'd never hurt another human being." She straightened her shoulders, let out a sigh. "And I felt glad."

"But what about poor Oliver Hutchins, the show-judge? What did he do to you? Poor guy probably didn't even know you."

"Yes, I admit, the stuffy old guy was probably only another one of Petra's victims." Sharon changed the gun into her other hand and frowned. "But when he got up to dance and left his jacket hanging there on the back of his chair, I thought, hey, this is too good an opportunity to miss. So, I twisted the button off his jacket and used it to frame him. Worked too. The police thought they'd found Petra's killer and closed the case." She raised her eyebrows in mock praise. "And you and your little detective team cooperated so well by proving his guilt for me."

When I didn't respond to her snide remark, she shrugged, continued. "Okay, I didn't set out to kill the show judge, but it had to be done. At the hotel, I pretended to be room service, put the gun to his head while he wasn't looking, and shot him. And then I sat down to email his confession to every name in his contact list." A smile lit her face. "Rather clever move, I thought."

"Except I've told the police Oliver couldn't have written that email. They weren't his words in the confession. Oliver wrote old-fashioned proper English. No way would he joke and say, 'orange doesn't suit me'."

Her frown deepened. "Yeah…the case was closed, I was away free, and then you and your nosey friends had to go around asking questions, stirring up the case, making the police investigate further." She spun around, her gun waving in the air. "And that's why I need to kill you. Once you're gone, your friends will realize they'll be next if they continue to ask questions."

I let out a snort. "You obviously do *not* know my friends. Kill me, and they'll hunt you down like the rat you are until you're locked in a four by four cell with nothing but a bucket to pee in for the rest of your natural life."

"Not if I threaten to kill the munchkins?"

Jake and Kayla.

My blood ran cold. I'd never understood that term before but with the icy chill that threatened to shut down my entire system, now I did.

"I know which day-care center the mouthy-one sends her children to," she continued, every word lashing my heart. "Easy enough to entice one or both out through the gate with pretty baubles."

This had gone far enough. I was not going to let this monster force me into a car and drive me out into the bush to dispose of me. I had to act. Now.

Pretending to give in to fear, I buried my face in my hands, made my shoulders shake as though it was all too much for me and I'd succumbed to tears. All the time watching her every movement with completely dry eyes. If she got away with killing me, I knew Dana and Molly would push the investigation to its limit, finally work out that Sharon was the killer and act. But what if Sharon enticed Jake away by taking his battered Doggo away? What if she talked Kayla into her car with a basketful of baby kittens?

And I wouldn't be around to stop her.

Sharon was standing by the window, twitching a curtain and peering outside. Probably checking to see if the coast was clear. No witnesses to see her force me into the car so she could make me drive out to the country, kill me, then run my car over a cliff with my body inside.

While she was distracted, I tensed my muscles ready to hurl myself across the room and slam into her body in an attempt to relieve her of her weapon.

But she spun around before I was even halfway out of the chair, arm held stiff in front of her, gun cocked. "Make my day," she growled sounding as much like Dirty Harry as Daisy Duck in drag. "Now get on your feet and head for the front door. I'll be right behind you and my finger is itchy."

I let out a deep sigh. Maybe I could drive the car into a brick wall and kill the both of us. At least that way she couldn't hurt Jake or Kayla – or anyone else for that matter.

With both wrists handcuffed together, I fumbled with the handle before opening the door and stepping out onto the verandah.

"Head toward the car," she instructed, her hot breath on my neck. "You on the driver's side. Me sitting right behind you with the gun two inches away from the back of your head. And then we'll take that little trip I promised you."

Not going to happen. The moment I climbed into my car I was a dead woman.

I scanned the area around the house. Not a soul in sight. I glanced along the road. Two cars parked in front of the house four doors up.

My eyes widened in recognition while my heart, already hammering like bongo drums in the jungle, switched to an even wilder tango beat.

Molly's little red Mini Cooper and Dana's SUV with its *Hydro Hound* trailer hitched on behind.

From this distance the cars appeared empty. But if Molly and Dana weren't in their cars, where were they?

Hiding nearby?

Inside one of the houses?

I gave a quick glance around and that's when I noticed the silver *Lexus* parked in the driveway over the road.

Nathan?

A sharp pain shot across my back as the barrel of Sharon's gun dug deep between my shoulder blades. "My finger's getting antsy," she snarled, "so no sudden moves. Now, very slowly, into the car!"

Not going to happen. She may as well shoot me here as send me to a fiery death over the side of a cliff. With my friends somewhere nearby – target practice for the crazy gunwoman if they showed their faces – I'd have to act now. Or I'd never see any of my loved ones again.

Was that a movement inside the carport? With the roller-door three-quarters of the way down, I couldn't see underneath.

Sharon must have heard the noise too. I felt the gun move away from that burning spot in the middle of my back and instinctively point in the direction of the movement.

Now...

With a warrior-like cry, I stepped back, smashed one Cuban heel down hard on Sharon's sneaker-clad foot, kicked backwards until I connected with a solid, but vulnerable shin bone and as she bent forward in pain, sent a well-sharpened elbow up into her chin, followed immediately by another into the stomach. A pain-filled *Oof!* was closely followed by a litany of seaman-worthy oaths that streamed from her open mouth, swear words that would have even made the pirate Blackbeard's hair curl.

What happened after that was a bit of a blur.

The gun went off, annihilating the head of my two-hundred-dollar dachshund statue that had previously sat in pride of place in the middle of my front lawn. The roller door sprung open with a clang. And four policemen, brandishing guns, batons and tasers, streamed out from under the door.

"This is the police! Put your gun on the ground and move away! Now!"

Sharon, clutching her stomach and hopping around on one foot, hissed out another barrage of swear-words before she dropped the gun and lifted both hands in the air.

Within seconds, *Pussy Willow* was face-down on the ground, her gun confiscated, my handcuffs off and I was being lifted bodily by a strong pair of arms and relocated to the grass in front of my English box hedge.

It was Nathan. Eyes wide, expression a mixture of anguish and relief. "Abi? You okay? Did she hurt you?" His voice cracked as he eyed me up and down, possibly checking for bullet holes. When I shook my head, he dragged me up against his chest, hard, and held on tight.

"But she planned to kill me," I told him through the wooly cashmere of his soft sweater pressed against my face. "Just like she killed Petra and Oliver."

His arms tightened another notch and I sagged against him like a balloon with the air escaping. It was all over. I sniffed. It felt so good wrapped in Nathan's arms, listening to his heartbeat, snuggled up against the safety of his rock-hard chest.

That's when Molly, eyes wide, hair standing on end, popped up from behind the box hedge. She was quickly followed by a grinning Dana.

"Molly? Dana?"

Molly, bottom lip trembling, wiped at her eyes with the back of her hand. "Hey, we did good, didn't we?"

"Oh, God yes, you did *very* good." I left the comfort of Nathan's arms and threw myself at my two friends, hugging them both. "But how did you get here without Sharon spotting you?"

"We were extra cautious," declared Dana with a shrug.

Molly nodded. "After your cryptic text, we decided not to pull up in front of your house. Instead we parked further along the street and walked back. And then, when Dana noticed the yellow car in your carport, we immediately knew something wasn't right, so we crawled along the front of the house, peeped through your lounge room window and there was Sharon threatening you with a gun."

"I was all for throwing a dirty big rock through the window and knocking Sharon out, but Molly thought it was too dangerous."

"It was. Sharon's gun was pointing straight at Abi's head."

"Yeah, but I still think I could have taken her out. People don't call me

Dead-Eye Dana for nothing."

"Dead-Eye Dana?" Molly grinned, eyes wide and disbelieving. "*What* people?"

Dana shrugged. "Well…the kids in the lane behind the house when I was little. I always knocked the most bottles off the fence when we had stone throwing competitions."

Still grinning at Dana, Molly shook her head, and then turned back to me. "Anyway, instead of letting Dana take aim, we got help. I rang Nathan while Dana rang the police."

"And here we are," added Nathan, snagging my arm and pulling me closer to tuck me up against him.

"I love you guys." I sniffed, fighting back tears. These three were the best friends any girl could have.

"Hey, looks like a police car heading this way. Came out of a driveway up the street where they've been hiding. Seems like our friend, *Pussy Willow* is in for an escorted ride to the police station."

"Where I hope she spends the rest of her life."

I let out a deep sigh and another noisy sniff. "It's over, isn't it?"

Molly nodded.

"Sharon can't hurt us anymore?"

"Nope," said Dana with a wink. "And the *Gumshoe Chicks* have solved another mystery."

21

With Mimi hanging tenaciously off my right leg, teeth enmeshed in the leather of my boot, I anchored the last two helium balloons onto the table decoration, purple ones to match the pink, green, yellow and blue balloons already hovering near the ceiling. It was a week after I'd come within a whisker of being blown away via a bullet from Sharon's gun and Molly and Dana, my two BFF's, had decided we'd celebrate solving our first big mystery by having a barbie, with all the trimmings.

Satisfied with the table display, I called out to Molly. "Have those steaks reached room temperature yet?"

"Yep. *And* the sausages. *And* the patties. You *do* know you have far too much food? Were you planning on inviting the entire street to this barbecue?"

The other *Gumshoe Chick*, Dana, wandered into the kitchen from the lounge room where she'd been changing her son's diaper, keeping the dogs away from the food and setting up more chairs. "It's the same with the cakes and finger-food. We'll have enough over to feed the homeless for a week. Peter's already been in and pinched a couple of the pastries, Jake's snagged a handful of chocolates and I found Kayla licking the icing off a green frog-cake. But even their pilfering hasn't put a dent in the spread."

There was a knock on the front door.

"That must be Nathan." I quickly ran my fingers through my hair and felt a wide grin tugging at my lips.

"Yeah. Must be." Molly's answering grin came with an eyebrow lift. Dana merely rolled her eyes.

"Coming!" As I hurried to the front door, I tried to shake Mimi off my leg for the umpteenth time. Fair dinkum, that dog would try the patience of Mother Teresa. Every outfit I wore had to include thick socks and boots to minimize the damage to my ankles and calves from her sharp snapping teeth.

"Mimi! Get off me!" As I walked, I continued to shake my leg, but her teeth were so embedded into to my right boot I could already feel the sharp points scratching my skin.

The little dog hated me, yet when the RSPCA came to pick her up after Sharon's sudden departure to prison, they had trouble catching her. Snarling and snapping like a whirling dervish, they ended up capturing her in a net. But the wild-eyed screams and full-on snarling told me they would never find a home for her, so I told them to leave her with me.

Ungrateful critter bit my finger so hard two minutes after they left, she made it bleed.

"Nathan, glad you could make it. Come in." A warm feeling caressed my insides as I smiled up into the face of the new man in my life. "Ignore the fluffy rat fastened to my leg. It's just Mimi. She hates me."

Nathan passed me a bottle of wine and a king-sized box of chocolates before squatting down to pat the little dog. "Hey, Mimi, girl. Remember me?"

She evidently did, because after unfastening her teeth from my leg, she looked up at Nathan, let out a series of excited yaps and her whole body began to wag. A smile lit up her face as she threw herself into his arms. It was magic. A complete metamorphosis. In the time it took to say *Remember me* Mimi changed from a pea-sized Tyrannosaurus into a tail-wagging angel, still dressed in her by-now, grubby tutu. In the time she'd been here I'd valued my fingers too much to attempt to disrobe her.

Meanwhile, Nathan, with Mimi wriggling happily in his arms, leant across and locked lips with me in a gentle kiss that had my legs threatening to buckle, before continued on into the kitchen. "Hey, looks great in here. How many have you invited? The whole neighborhood?"

"No. Just Molly, Dana, you, Pete, the kids and the dogs. If there's any food left over it can always be eaten tomorrow."

Molly, wiping soot from her nose wandered into the kitchen. "And you haven't even seen the pile of meat she's got outside for the barbecue. We'll be eating cold cuts for the rest of the week."

"G'day mate." Peter, Dana's husband, popped his head around the back door before strolling inside to collect two barbecue aprons hanging over the kitchen sink. "Ready to man the barbie?" He held up the two aprons for Nathan's perusal. "Which one do you want? *'Kiss the Chef'* or *'You Kill It We'll Cook It'*?"

"Not much to think about there," said Nathan snaffling *'Kiss the Chef'*. He placed Mimi down on the floor and when she whined her objection, gently scratched behind her ears. He then stood up and while slipping the apron over his head, leaned forward to plant another kiss on my lips.

Ahhh. I knew there was a reason I 'd bought that apron.

Peter grinned. "Okay, mate, let's go show the womenfolk exactly how to grill the perfect steak."

"You're on." Nathan rubbed his hands together. "My steaks will go down in history for their amazing flavor and chewability. So," he raised an eyebrow at me, "to help me create my masterpiece, I'll need chilli, curry-powder–"

"No need," I told him, lifting my nose in mock superiority. "The steaks have already been marinated in soy sauce, olive oil, lemon juice, Worcestershire sauce, garlic power, basil, parsley and pepper."

"Wow!" His grin was slow with a hint of wicked, sending warm signals to all areas below my waistline. "Sounds *hot!*"

"Um…" For a moment I didn't know whether I was up, down, coming or going. I cleared my throat and gulped, hoping my face wasn't as flushed and out of control as my thoughts.

Dana leaned over and snaffled a carrot stick from a colored jar on the table. "Want us to go outside and leave you two alone for ten minutes?" She slid the carrot stick in her mouth and began to chew.

Feeling heat rip through my cheeks and down my neck, I grabbed two barbecue spatulas from the drawer under the sink and handed them to Nathan and Peter. "Okay, guys, start cooking," I said, ignoring the amusement in Nathan's eyes. "And I want those steaks to melt in the mouth. Okay?"

With a laugh, Nathan nodded then looked down at the dog at his feet. Intent on getting back into his arms, Mimi was bouncing up and down attempting to climb up his leg. "Sorry, Mimi, no can do. I have meat to cook. You can come outside with Pete and me if you like, but no pinching any sausages. Right?"

It was a couple of hours later, after the pile of food had been demolished and we sat stretched out on canvas chairs in the backyard, drinks beside us, that the conversation turned to our latest mystery and my close call with death.

"Okay," said Dana confiscating a garden snail from Jake's fingers seconds before the snail disappeared into his mouth. "What have we learned from this investigation?"

"Don't annoy anyone who owns a gun?" Molly waved her second glass of wine in the air for emphasis. Liquid sloshed over the edge and I immediately decided to make two wines her quota for the night.

"Maybe we should keep in contact with each other more during an investigation," I suggested thinking of the useless text I'd sent the other two when I knew Sharon was after me. Why didn't I mention her name?

Peter frowned. "And what about the elephant in the room? Abi nearly died."

"Don't you think we know that?" said Dana. "Which is why we need to learn from our mistakes."

"Well, I think you should give up on this *Gumshoe Chick* thing. "

"Geez, mate," put in Nathan rolling his eyes at his friend. "Are you looking to sleep in the spare room tonight?"

"Gumshoe Chick *thing*?" Dana's voice crackled with ice as she glared at her husband. "Nathan's right, except as we have no spare room, until you apologize, Peter Sullivan, you own the sofa."

"But I only meant it's dangerous. I worry about you."

"Still sleeping on the sofa."

"Okay, okay, I'm sorry, but at least promise to be careful." He did a poor imitation of a doe-eyed dog face. Looked more like he had indigestion. "'Cos I love you, honey-pie."

"Of course, we'll be careful." The ice in Dana's voice showed signs of thawing as Peter's arm snaked out and drew her closer.

"Maybe when I'm not busy with paid work I can lend a hand uncovering any classified information you might need in the future," said Nathan, suppressing a grin as he watched the interaction between Dana and Peter.

"See," growled Dana smacking Peter on the arm. "Nathan doesn't think women are too fragile to make good detectives. Tonight's a celebration. The *Gumshoe Chicks* have just solved their first adult mystery." She picked up her glass and raised it in the air. "To us. To the *Gumshoe Chicks*. May we solve more mysteries than Nancy Drew and Miss Marple combined."

I took a sip of my wine. Smiled at Dana and Molly. What would I do without my two best friends? Since Sharon's attempt to kill me, nightmares had plagued my dreams. Sharon, dressed in her pole-dancing costume and carrying a gun as big as a motorcycle dancing around me, singing a dirge, taunting me, explaining in colorful detail how much it would hurt when a bullet ripped through my flesh and took out my heart. Sharon, holding Mimi in one arm and a blazing gun in the other, dressed in nothing but cowboy boots and a black cowboy hat pulled down over one eye as she lined me up and used me for target practice.

And it was the quick thinking of my two best friends that saved me. Not the person on the other end of my phone. *Joe's Pizza*, who I'd rung the night before to make an order. Joe had picked up, thought someone was playing a trick on him and promptly hung up again.

"You okay, Abi?" Nathan, sitting beside me, squeezed my hand.

"Yeah, fine." I smiled down at Mimi, Sharon's little hell-fire dog curled up on Nathan's lap, a blissful expression on her face and suddenly thought of Petra's little pug. Happily, she'd been rehomed with Petra's grandmother who lived by herself and was looking for companionship.

Mimi, looked so sweet on Nathan's lap. So angelic. I reached out to pat her. Immediately the blissful expression turned into that of an ugly supernatural goblin. All snarls and sharp fangs. Quickly withdrawing my fingers from danger, I let out sigh. It was like the little dog blamed me for Sharon's incarceration. "Mimi hates me."

"She's probably only missing her owner," said Molly, licking the rim of her glass after draining the last drop. "She'll be okay once she realizes you're the one who provides her food."

I shook my head. "It's almost like she blames me for Sharon going away and leaving her motherless."

"Come on, Abs, dogs aren't logical," said Dana.

I had my doubts about that.

Nathan, tickling Mimi under the chin, grinned when the little fluffball began purring like a cat. "You know, she can always come live with me."

"Who? Mimi?" I frowned at Nathan. Was he teasing me?

"Yeah. It's time I had another dog."

"You mean that?"

"Of course." He looked up and grinned. "As long as you promise to babysit for me when I have to go out of town."

"Any time." Geez, I'd even pay for her special Doggy Do kibble and provide her with Gucci dog clothes if he was serious.

He leaned closer and whispered in my ear, so softly, I had to strain to hear his words. So seductively, I had to bite my tongue to stop from moaning. "And can I bring Mimi with me when I stay here overnight?"

I tipped my head up so his lips could meld with mine.

Stay overnight?

Ooh…yeah…

Dear Readers

GONE TO THE DOGS is the first book in my new series, the *Gumshoe Chick Mysteries*. There are three *Chicks* – Abigail Truelove, Molly Gibson and Dana Fox. All dog-show competitors. All 28-year-old Nancy-Drew-wannabees. All owners of pampered pooches. If you've enjoyed reading GONE TO THE DOGS, why not pop over to Amazon, or whichever online store you bought this book from and leave an honest review? Reviews are like dessert for authors. In fact, they are part of what keeps me writing – knowing you've spent time with the characters I created, dressed up and injected with life. Especially for you.

www.junewhytebooks.com.

I'd also like to acknowledge and thank those who have helped me in my writing journey. My beta readers, Nancy, June K and Bev – couldn't do without you. My forever friends, Robyn and Wendy – I know I can always whip off an email with a question or ask for a second opinion and it will be answered with a smile. And Traci Andrighetti, USA bestselling author of the *Franki Amato Mysteries*, whose suggestions and edits made this book the best it could be.

Thank you,

June Whyte